Praise for *Vampire Conditions*

At turns dark and brutal and wickedly funny, Brian Allen Carr's *Vampire Conditions* will put you in mind of Hannah, Pancake, Powell. This book will grab you by the throat and knock the wind out of you, will make you want to drive south, raise hell, hide out, call home, tell your friends.

—**Robert Lopez**

Vampire Conditions melds a precise Texas regional with gothic, recalling Flannery O'Connor, who wrote out of Georgia. But Carr's intricate narrative patterns, jump cuts and unanticipated segues, along with his evocative drawings, have a distinctly postmodern feel. Any way you cut it, Brian Allen Carr is a potently eccentric writer.

—**Harold Jaffe**

Praise for Brian Allen Carr

Winner of the inaugural 2011 Texas Observer Story Prize as judged by Larry McMurtry.

A finalist for the 2011 Texas Institute of Letters Steven Turner Award for First Fiction.

"Brian Allen Carr's brain must be a snarl of firing pistons, sizzling fuses, hoses leaking blood and tequila and hydraulic oil. How else can you explain the twisted machinery of his stories? Each of them a disturbing journey that will thrill and educate you in the sunlit haze of the Texas/Mexico border– and the sometimes subterranean darkness of the human heart."

—**Benjamin Percy**, author of *The Wilding*

"These stories are everything hardworking–the characters, the scenery, the sentences–all form to build a machine crafted to break hearts along the border. A ridiculously strong first collection."

—**Shane Jones**, author of *Light Boxes*

"*Short Bus* balances the harshness of characters' lives with beautiful and precise language, making parched land feel lush. Carr writes the best kind of stories-stories that only he could have written."

—**Mary Miller**, author of *Big World*

HOLLER PRESENTS

Vampire Conditions
2012

VAMPIRE CONDITIONS

A Holler Presents Collection

BRIAN ALLEN CARR

Vampire Conditions
Copyright 2012 Brian Allen Carr
All Rights Reserved
First Edition: June 2012
Manufactured in the United States
ISBN 13: 978-0983258902

Front Cover Design by Matthew Revert
Book layout by David McNamara / sunnyoutside

Stories from Vampire Conditions originally appeared in
these publications:
"The Paint from her Hands" — Kitty Snacks issue 4,
"Lucy Standing Naked" — Fiction International issue
48, "The First Henley" — Texas Observer, "Corrido"
— New Border: An Anthology of Texas/Mexico Border
Writing, "A Brief OK" — Hobart issue 13, "Everything
will Fall its Way" — The Puritan issue 16

Holler Presents
110 Hale Street
Beckley, WV
25801

scottmcclanahan@hotmail.com
hollerpresents@gmail.com

Boy's Town #1

Boy's Town #2

Boy's Town #3

Slug Trail #2

Boy's Town #1

His suit looked toy-store made, and his eyes seemed sugar loaded. He stood on the street corner and called to us singingly. "Five dollar pussy wagon," he said, each word wrapped in petals of music, "fucky-fucky. Sucky-suck. I'll take you to another place where money counts as luck. You don't have to be pretty for your soul to house a shame. Come along. Come along. Get inside." We'd been looking for him, but he still came as a shock to us. His posture was regal—three or four of his teeth capped with gold. There dangled a chain from his neck. He stood beside a flat-maroon Lincoln. He flung open the rear-passenger door. It sang like a rusty spring. We nodded and lowered ourselves against the sun-smoothed interior. We expected the car to smell like cigarette ash or food heavy with onions. Instead, it had a flavor not unlike cinnamon gum.

THE PAINT FROM
HER HANDS

When the baby came dead they held her for a few hours on the kitchen floor with their legs tangled in the purged amniotic fluid, and Tabitha cried with her head thrown back against the refrigerator door, but Barrow didn't say a thing. He even breathed quiet, drawing the burnt-almond scented air through his nose, his thoughts as puzzled as dust floating in light. They had been to the flea market the week before and had seen a woman with a stand where she made dolls in the likeness of real babies for mementos, and they had smiled and laughed with her and had said they'd see her in a few weeks, and the doll maker held her hand against Tabitha's belly and said, "I'll wait for the day." Wait for the day? Barrow and Tabitha had walked away from her stand smiling and holding hands, but that was last week. An hour of blue-colored silence followed the birth. "Barrow," Tabitha said, "Barrow?" Her shoulders shook and so did her voice, her tears muddling her throat, so Barrow's name lowed from her achingly. "What we gonna?" she said. "Barrow, what we gonna do?" Gonna do? Gonna do? Barrow stumbled the phrase through his mind as he thumbed the small thing's lips, smooth beneath his weathered finger. Gonna do? He thumbed the lips. Gonna do? Its face like a pebble. He'd heard they'd come that way. Like statues unmoving that drew breaths and became themselves. But this one hadn't breathed. It was still when its face hit the light; it stayed still as he dragged the umbilical cord across his blade. He put a thumb against one of its cold, tiny palms, and Tabitha watched Barrow's lips. Then Barrow stood, baby in hand. "Barrow?" Tabitha said. Nothing. "Barrow?" He shook his head. "Barrow?" He couldn't look at her. "Barrow?" Fluid spat from the soles of his shoes as he exited the kitchen.

/ / /

The trees in the orchard beyond the yard of their home were heavy with green grapefruit. They'd ripen in the weeks to come and grow pale orange out from the stem. Summer was coming. The heat brought sweat to Barrow's chest within a dozen steps, and his shirt stuck to him. He lowered a strap from his coveralls. He set the baby in the yard. He ran his hands down his shirt undoing the buttons. He flung the shirt into the grass. He re-shouldered his coverall strap. He picked up the baby. The plum-colored cord dangled loose from its belly. Barrow walked toward a row of the orchard. Thirteen months back, he and Tabitha had stood in the grass with ripe fruit in piles about them, the perfume of the citrus cutting the damp air. It was an earlier growing season, and they'd hired a half-dozen Mexicans to pick. The Mexicans had run out of boxes and had made mounds of grapefruit in the grass, and Tabitha had taken a grapefruit and set it on her head, and told Barrow, "I bet you can't hit it," and Barrow pulled his revolver from his holster and shot the fruit clean off her skull from ten yards away. One of the Mexicans crossed himself when he saw the juice spray in the air, shaking his head when the rind came down a moment or so later, and then the air was hot with gunpowder, and Tabitha laughed and laughed and rubbed her burgeoned belly, filled with a baby that hadn't made it either.

Barrow's feet sank in the soft earth with each step down the row. He kept an orgone accumulator at the center of his orchard. He had built it using a schematic a poet friend had sent him in the mail. "It'll unshrink you," the poet friend had written, and Barrow had spent an hour in the box every day since its construction some eight months back. He opened the pine door and stepped into the sheet-iron lined box. He sat down on the stool inside. He cradled the baby in his arms. He closed the accumulator door, and the space around him darkened.

/ / /

Barrow couldn't make out her words when she reached him. He heard her palm strike the accumulator door. The accumulator thumped like a drum, and Tabitha's dampened voice swam through the dark. He touched the baby's cheek to his own. It was soft and chill. He wished it warm. He put his palm against the door. Was the box rebuilding him? Could it rebuild the baby? He pressed the door open. It swung soft. Outside Tabitha held tight to a grapefruit-tree branch with one hand. With the other hand she held her dirtied-white gown bunched beside her. Her legs trembled. Her face was damp and pale. Her toes clenched the dirt. "What we gonna do?" She asked.

Barrow dragged Tabitha back toward the house. He slung her arm over his shoulder and held the baby in his free arm. Tabitha's feet caught against the dirt. Barrow looked at her face. Her eyes closed. He dragged her back to the yard and laid her in the grass. He found his flung shirt. He spread it open. He laid the still baby on the shirt and it looked like a shadow, and one of its eyes glazed open, and Barrow flipped the lid closed with a finger, crossed its arms and wrapped it up in a bundle. He lifted Tabitha from the grass and hoisted her to his shoulder. He lifted the bundled baby in his palm. He carried them both into the house. He took Tabitha to the back room. He lit a candle that smelled of lavender. He went to the kitchen and ran cold water over a wash cloth. He rang the cloth. Beads of water drummed the sink. He went back to the bedroom. He folded the cloth over twice and spread it across Tabitha's brow. She took angry, unconscious breaths. Barrow looked into the bundle. Still the child was still and colored dimly. Barrow knew the place to go.

/ / /

The woman at the market cracked an egg open and emptied it into her hand. She dropped the shell into the soil of a potted hibiscus on the ground beside her, and she spread her fingers and tilted her palm and let the egg white slip into a metal mixing bowl. She then slid the yolk into a granite molcajete and took up a pestle and swirled it through the yolk before raising and mashing the bright yellow sack with the dull instrument. She had already formed the face from polymer clay. She had looked down upon the still baby as her thumbs worked the soft mound. She pulled a body from the shelf. It was intact, a small cloth abdomen with plastic arms and legs. The arms and legs were near-ivory white. She took a canister of powdered lapis lazuli from a cabinet behind her. She scooped a measure of the blue powder and sprinkled it into the yolk and she added other powders and mashed the paste, and Barrow watched the woman and then looked at the baby's face. He watched the woman and then looked at the baby's face. A chime rang and the woman reached for the small oven door and pulled it open. She grabbed a pair of tongs from the table beside her, took the memento-baby's head from the oven and laid it on a cooling rack on a separate work station. The woman then looked at Barrow. She looked at the gun which he'd pulled from his pocket the moment he'd reached her stand. She reached for the rich blue paint in the molcajete. Barrow cocked his gun. "Want it to look right don't ya?" the woman said. Barrow shook his head. "The face," the woman said as she picked up the molca-jete, "the same blue." Then Barrow shot the paint from her hands and took the white memento-child away from her.

/ / /

Barrow laid both babies in the passenger seat of his pickup and drove out to a bluff overlooking the river. He parked the car near an olive tree and got down and grabbed a narrow-bladed shovel from the bed of the truck and dug a hole where a mass of fallen white blossoms had landed and turned the color of tobacco. The ground was soft and the shovel blade passed with the softest press from his boot, and it only took a few scoops to go a foot down, and it needed to be so narrow that the grave was dug in just a few minutes, and he was able to lay the still baby down in the soft black dirt. He'd been to a funeral or two in the past. He always liked to listen to the ministers. He liked to hear them talk about the people in the coffins. He liked to hear about them flying off to heaven. Barrow didn't know whether or not babies went to heaven, but he wished a minister was there to tell him they did. He wished there was somebody there to say something, but it was quiet except for the sound of the slow river in the distance. He watched the water for a moment moving. Then Barrow covered the thing with the soft mound of unearthed soil beside him and headed home.

/ / /

Barrow had to shake Tabitha awake, and when she came to, she'd forgotten a moment, Barrow could tell by the peace in her face, and then the reality came awake in her, and her eyes tightened in the corners. Again she asked Barrow what they should do, and again Barrow was quiet. He looked down at his lap. Tabitha looked down too. Barrow had bundled the fake baby in a small cotton blanket. He picked it up in his hands. He shrugged his shoulders and looked at Tabitha, and Tabitha pulled at the edge of the blanket, and it fell open just enough to show the ivory face. Shock filled Tabitha. She touched the thing's head with the tip of a fingernail. Her nail clicked against the skin of it, and she nodded and looked at Barrow who had wet in his eyes. Tabitha leaned back against her pillow. She opened her arms. Barrow laid the baby in them, and Tabitha pulled it to her chest. She looked down at it. She asked it questions that Barrow didn't understand, but Barrow could see from Tabitha's expression that the baby had a silent way of answering her. The thing's actions could solve riddles. He could since a logic in its stillness. And Barrow let a smile take him gently, because he knew he'd found his kin.

LUCY STANDING NAKED

Lucy Colon kissed at strangers in the hall. She'd hold her face cold and still as winter concrete for the most part, but when she neared the strangers, got a step away, she'd turn her face toward them, pucker up, and suck a kiss through her lips. Most strangers wouldn't even notice. Some would turn their heads unsure. Others might flinch at the sound, brushing their ears with their finger tips as though shooing away a fly. I only knew because she told me. Well, at first. At first she told me, and I sort of shrugged it off, but then I saw. Watched her kiss at a stranger. Watched Lucy crack a kiss toward a chubby boy's ear, and watched the boy's face go perplexed, his eyelids cinching slightly around his eyes. I stopped him. "What just happened?" I asked. "Huh?" he said. "When you walked by that girl?" I said, and he and I watched Lucy prance down the hall and he touched the ear that had been toward her and said, "I don't know," and then, "but maybe something."

/ / /

This is how I met Lucy: My parents bought the house down the street from her. *This is the season my parents bought the house:* summer. *This is the city the house was in:* Corpus Christi, Texas.

This was our first full conversation:

"You live there?" I asked and pointed to her house. A shaggy thing. Sort of a shadow of a home sunk back into tall grass.

"Yeah," she said.

A car drove by.

"You live there?" she asked and pointed to my house, as my father carried a box toward the front door, whistling as he looked up into the thicket of branches climbing lazily from the live oaks.

"Yeah," I said.

We both kind of nodded.

This was the first time I saw Lucy standing naked:

The streets in Corpus Christi are black asphalt, and in the summers they go sticky and soft, and you feel your shoes might become a part of them as you walk along kicking rocks. There are always rocks to kick in Corpus Christi. There are always rocks to kick and shirtless people with tattoos. I was kicking rocks and pulling pigweeds from the cracks in the road when I'd come to them. I didn't know a soul, so my parents told me to go walking, "Bound to run into someone your age," they said. I did, but not in their way. We were a block from the bay. A dirty salty puddle really, but most bays are.

Bays are not beautiful up close. From far away and in pictures they are beautiful. Up close it's like clear vomit. Little bits of dead things bobbing around in the ebbs. Sometimes I'd walk the asphalt down. At the edge of the bay stood cement steps. At the bottom of the steps, a small beach of oyster shells. Most broken to bits so small you could swallow them. Lucy was down there the first time I went, her shirt off. She was flopping around in the salt water, hanging off the arm of a tattooed fella who looked twice her age. She had bracelets on. Dozens of bracelets.

This was our second full conversation:

"Why didn't you get in with us?"

"Get in where?"

"You don't have to play dumb. Want a cigarette?"

I told her I did, but when she lifted the lighter I said I wanted to save mine for after dinner, because I heard that was when they were best, and she nodded and we both stuck the cigarettes behind our ears.

"You Chinese?" she asked.

"Not sure," I told her.

/ / /

My father is a butcher, my mother is a secretary, my grandmother was an accountant and she paid for some of the house.

I don't know what I want to be when I grow up. The first day of school they asked that. They said there wasn't much time. I'm fourteen years old. They say I need to get with the program. I don't know what the program is, but I imagine it's a gray thing and probably it's large.

My father wants me to be a country western singer. "There's never been one like you," he told me. He bought me a guitar and taught me some chords, and in the evening, when he's stretched out on the patio drinking Lone Stars, he has me bring it out and strum songs, and he sings along with me, in a sort of gravelly whisper, staring out into nothing as I tumble through the saddest of tunes.

/ / /

Lucy told me I should kiss at strangers too. This was a few weeks into school. "It's a rush, kinda," she said.

"What if they notice?"

"That's when it's best."

Lucy had green nail polish and black nail polish and pink nail polish and orange nail polish and blue. She had all of these polishes on at the same time.

"I saw you with your guitar," she told me.

"Where?"

"Through your window."

"You looked in my window?"

"Why not?"

I shrugged.

"You write your own songs?"

"Not really."

"You should. You should write a song about a man who gets his legs chopped off and about a blind woman who has to take care of him."

"I don't know," I said. "Seems unrealistic."

"It's not either," she said. "It's a true story. I saw it on the TV. And people like true stories. They like things that's real."

/ / /

"You're adopted," my mother told me on my twelfth birthday. She said I was old enough to know. She said, "Surely you noticed." I did. I don't know from what country, but I know that I'm Asian. I have Asian eyes and Asian hair. And one time a bully asked me if it sucked, and I asked him if what sucked, and he said, having a little Asian dick. I didn't know if I had a little Asian dick or not, because I'd not seen enough dicks to know. I'd never seen my dad's dick even, but I figured his was bigger than mine, but he's a dad. Back then, when I'd take a piss in a busy bathroom, I'd try to see the other dicks at the other stalls from the corner of my eye, but it was hard to tell. You couldn't just turn and look, and everything looks the same out of the corner of your eye. It looks blurry.

I didn't get mad at my mom when she told me I was adopted on my twelfth birthday. Mainly because she had already told me on my eleventh birthday. And on my tenth birthday. And on my ninth. On my eighth birthday, though, that time was different. That time I cried and cried.

/ / /

This was the first time Lucy and I kissed: It was after Halloween and the streets smelled like busted pumpkins.

"Wanna make out?" she asked as we sat on a curb. She was dressed like a nun, and I was dressed like a cowboy.

"I don't know," I said. I had used my hat to collect candy, and I was looking through it to see what all I'd collected.

She blew smoke, "Ever done it?"

"All the time," I told her, and she laughed and said, "You're a liar."

I looked away. "How does it work?"

"Hold your mouth open," she said. I did. She leaned in close, and I kind of leaned back, but then she put her hand on the back of my head, and put her mouth up to mine and wagged her tongue against my tongue, and it tasted smoky and sweet and heavy and warm, and my fists were clenched so tight my fingers numbed, and my eyes were opened all the way.

/ / /

My grandmother can't believe I don't understand algebra. "It's the easiest math," she says.

"Easier than addition?" I say.

"Well, no," she says. "There's nothing easier than that."

I don't understand why they don't keep the numbers with the numbers and the letters with the letters, and I never really get why we're graphing what we're graphing. Some of the graphs look like this:

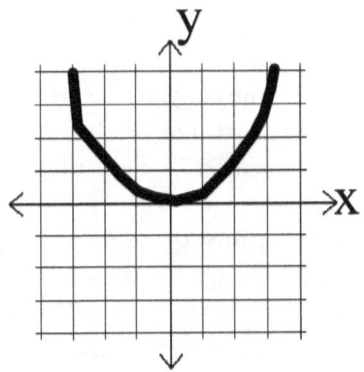

Most of the time in algebra I have to ask tons of questions, and everyone is always rolling their eyes at me and putting their heads down on their desks.

"Hey," this one kid said to me one day after the bell. "Hey, hey, hey."

I turned around and looked at him. I kind of lifted my glasses closer to my eyes and raised my backpack on my shoulders and sort of tilted my head and smiled.

"Do you know Kung Fu?" he asked.

I shook my head no. Then he punched me in the nose.

Algebra's the last class of the day, so I walked home with my face bloody, and my dad was already home when I got there. He had me sit in a chair, and he reached into the fridge. He pulled out a sirloin and laid it across my eyes. "Does it hurt?" he asked.

"It's cold."

"I mean where he got you," he said.

I pressed against the steak, and the steak pressed against my face. "It doesn't feel good."

/ / /

Lucy leaned against the tattooed fella, and the tattooed fella leaned against the wall. The two sat, legs fully extended, on the carpeted floor in Lucy's room. Both smoked cigarettes. The tattooed fella's eyes, limp as raw bacon, sort of shiny in their sockets and ribboned with red.

"Say something again," he told me.

"Like what?" I asked, and he began to laugh, and Lucy looked at him and said, "Don't be an asshole," but the tattooed fella buckled up with giggles, his face pink and squinted.

"I'm sorry," he said. "I just never seen a chink with a hick's voice."

This was the day after the sucker punch, and I wasn't in the mood for anything, so I went home and started getting ready for dinner. A couple of minutes later my dad threw open the door and danced into the kitchen. He did this a lot. He'd dance in on his way to the shower. He liked to "wash the meat off him" first thing. Most times he'd swing by my mother, who'd be slumped in her seat at the kitchen table, fiddling with a magazine, and he'd always try to hug her, but she'd press him away with a palm and say, "First wash the meat off," and then he'd dance away from her toward the shower, and you could hear him singing as the water hissed through the whole house, that hum that old pipes make, and then he'd come out wrapped in a towel, scraping an ear with a Q-tip, his upper half naked, a pale blot of hairy flesh, and this is what he did that day, though there was more spark to it. "Guess whose meat I cut today," he said. My mother didn't even look up from her magazine, and I barely turned away from the potatoes I was washing. "Whose?" I said. My dad came over and drummed his palms on my shoulder, and I dropped the wet potato I'd been holding, and it pounded around in the sink. "Buddy Straight's," he said.

My mom looked up from her magazine, but not at my father. She puzzled her face at the ceiling for a moment and then looked back down. "Who?" she said, her voice aimed at the pages.

"Buddy Straight," my dad said, and he looked at me, as though I'd know the name he was saying. "Straight," he said. "George Straight," his voice hammering down the last name.

"Buddy Straight's George Straight?" my mother said.

My father shook his head. He sort of pounced lightly on the balls of his bare feet toward her. "His brother," my father said.

I flipped the water back on, and scrubbed at a grungy potato eye. "Cool," I said.

My father slicked his wet hair back to his skull, and flung beads of water at the floor. "More than *cool*," he said. "It could be our in."

"In?" my mother said.

"Yes, sir," my dad said, and then he screamed, "Woo Hoo!" and my grandmother called out from deep within the house, "What's going on?" and then my father hollered back, "Nelson's gonna be famous!"

My father beamed at me, and my grandmother made her way toward the kitchen. I could hear her walker clicking across the terrazzo. "What, what?" she asked as she got to the door.

"Just some foolishness," my mother said, and she shirked away her magazine and launched into another. "Timmy's taking a thing too far."

"What?" my dad said, and he sort of danced over to me, tucking tighter at his towel. "I don't think I'm taking it too far at all."

"He met George Straight's brother," I said to my grandmother, and I flipped off the faucet and dried my hands on a towel. "Nothing major." My grandmother looked confused.

"Nothing major," my father said. "Hell," he said, "everyone knows that Buddy works for his brother. The man's got an F-350 and no job. He does things for him, and I told him about you," my father chucked his Q-tip into the waste bin. "He came in ordering rib eyes, and I recognized a family resemblance, and so I sort of asked him about it, and he told me that sure enough, they was related, and not even just kind of related, but brothers and all that, and then I told him I had a boy with a gift," my father nudged me with an elbow, "and he said the country world was always looking out for young talent, and so I says you should come and see him, and I kind of snuck him some extra steaks, and he said he'd love to, and so I invited him over."

"Dammit, Timmy," my mother said. "If you get canned on account of stealing steaks, I swear I'll wring you."

"She's right," said my grandmother, as she creaked back toward her room. "I raised you better than that."

But my dad didn't seem to hear them, "So," he said and looked at me.

"So what?" I said.

"So you gotta get ready," he told me.

That night we spent hours on the patio practicing.

/ / /

29

"You done it yet?" Lucy asked.

"Done what?"

"Kissed at a stranger?"

We were leaned against our lockers and I was thumbing my swollen nose. Nothing aches like a punched nose. The whole thing feels poisoned, and when you press against it little lights flare behind your eyes. "No," I told her. "I don't think I will. I don't see a point." Then a gangly guy with a fresh haircut came walking by, and just as he passed Lucy kissed at his ear, and he brushed the side of his face as he went gawking down the hall.

Lucy poked my ribs. "If you keep messing with it, it'll take longer to heal."

I dropped my hands to my sides. "I gotta take a piss," I told her and walked down the hallway to the bathroom.

The bathroom at the high school was always humid. The mirrors were fogged up, and there was a hum and a hiss. Some undefinable and stale sound that you could hear with your whole body but couldn't find the source of with your eyes.

There were only two urinals with no dividers between them, and the gangly guy that Lucy kissed at was at one, and there was someone shitting in the only stall, so I had to piss beside him.

It always takes a long time to start pissing when you're that close to someone, and so while I was standing there, waiting for the piss to come, I tried catching a glimpse of the guy's dick from the corner of my eye, but just as I did that he flushed and pulled back, so the two of us met eyes a bit, and he kind of bucked up and said, "You looking at my dick?"

And I just shook my head no, and I still wasn't even pissing.

"You're not even pissing," he said.

"It's coming," I said. "It's in there."

"And earlier," he said. "In the hall," his face began to tighten. "Did you fucking kiss at me?"

"No," I told him. "Not me. Lucy."

"You fucking kissed at me, and came in to look at my dick," he said, and then I closed my eyes, because I thought he was gonna slug me, and I waited with my hands on my cock for a fist to land against my already throbbing nose. But when I opened them he was walking away. "Fucking pervert," he said. And then he went out the door. I can't remember if I pissed after that or not.

/ / /

In Algebra we're always solving for X. You have to move things around on both sides of the equation. You have to take this:

X+7*2= 15

And turn it into this:

X = 1

But I don't get the point of X in the first place. If you don't know what something is, just leave it alone. I had a teacher once who asked if I'd ever thought about trying to find my real parents, as though it was something I should do. There was that kind of tone in her voice, and until then I swear it hadn't occurred to me. I've gone to the library a few times and looked at books about Asia, and seen pictures of people from different countries, and read about cultures, but I sort of like not knowing exactly where I'm from. In Korea they've got music called Pansori, and the songs can be up to eight hours long. In Japan they've got a music called Min'yō where people chant like the blues. In Taiwan they've got Nanguan where women sing sadness over flutes piping behind them. I've never heard any of that music, not that I'm all that big on music anyhow. I guess the best part of music is that there's not much unknown. Especially in country, because it's always someone leaving or dying or drinking or fighting or loving the United States or talking about God, and the music's simple mostly. Just a few chords. A few notes. These stories about people getting banged around. These stories about hard working losers. And I guess that's the part my dad likes the best, because I've gone and seen him plenty at work. Watched him hang cows by their legs from the ceiling, and watched him find the bundles of muscles to be pulled away and cut up as steaks. All the red coming away clean in his nubby hands, a sort of gristled expression held heavy in his lower lip as he knifes the beef from the bone and lays it heavy on plastic boards for trimming. And at home the grind continues. My mom seems sick when she sees him. She doesn't like to talk to us she says, because she spends the whole day answering phones, and so she sits with her magazines while my father stretches out sipping Lone Stars and listens to me singing. Most times I don't even realize that he's not really mine and that I'm not really part of him. He smiles at me after I sing songs, and I know that he means it.

"How's your nose?" he asked me a few days after I'd been punched. I'd just played him a new song, and I sort of touched my face with my right hand as I slid my left hand up and down the neck of the guitar.

"It's healing," I told him.

/ / /

"Let's see it then," Lucy said.

"What?" I said.

She was sitting on the edge of her bed with her hands on her knees, and I was sitting on a chair by her desk scribbling on a piece of paper with a pen. She had asked me about the rumors. The gangly guy had told folks about the scene in the bathroom and about the kiss, and Lucy understood the kiss part, but she couldn't understand why I'd check him out at the urinal, and so I had to explain to her, and she laughed a bit and said she could tell me.

Said she'd, "seen enough dicks to know." We were listening to the Violent Femmes, and I'd wished there had been some other music on. Something slower. Something sad.

"Don't be afraid," she said. "I won't laugh or nothing." She leaned back into her pillows and put her hands behind her head. "And I'll keep my hands to myself."

I smiled and stood up. "Is the air conditioner on?" I asked.

"Warm?" she said.

My hands felt scraped out as I put them on my belt buckle. My lungs felt folded in half. I couldn't get any air into them. I could hear everything better. I tugged at my belt, and then unbuttoned my blue jeans, and I could hear the button come undone, and I don't think I'd ever heard it before. Everything is awkward when you're about to be naked in front of someone for the first time. My dick was as stiff as it could be, and it sort of helped the zipper to lower, and then I fished it out of my boxers, and it sort of heaved free, and bobbed up and down, as full a boner as I'd ever had.

"Shit," said Lucy.

I hid it with my hands, and she shot up on her bed.

"Don't hide it," she told me. She grabbed my wrists and held them away from me tight in her hands. She grinned big. "That's some cock," she said.

"Small?" I said.

And then she looked up at me, "Oh, no, Nelson," she said. "That's a thing to be proud of," and her eyes sort of glistened as I stuffed myself back into my pants.

"What time is it?" I asked.

She fanned her face with a hand and then looked at her watch. "Five thirty," she said.

"Fuck," I said, and I ran out of her room and out the front door and into the street, and I kicked a rock and it skipped at Buddy Straight's F-350 parked in front of the house, and I ran into the kitchen, and my father hollered, "Where the hell you been," but I just shrugged at him and then he said to Buddy, "Mr. Straight, I'd like to introduce you to my son," and Buddy squeezed my hand so hard it felt like my brain would burst against the back of my eyes.

"Hear you're a sanger," he said.

And my shoulders felt wider than they'd ever been, and I said, "Sure as hell am." And he and my father's faces scrunched up wild, and I grabbed my guitar from my mother, who was holding it and looking brightly at Buddy, sort of surveying the length of his purple sports coat, and I said, "Wanna hear a song?"

We sat on the patio. My father cracked beers. I'd never been so strong behind that wooden thing. The guitar seemed smaller to me, and I sang Buddy

a tune I'd been working over. I won't tell all of it,
but the chorus went like this:

> I lost my legs
> And you lost your eyes
> But the good lord helped us
> To make it on our way
> God bless the USA
> And open me a beer
> And then we will go dancing
> In my seeing-eye wheelchair

And when I was done my dad handed me a
fresh Lone Star and said, "Nelson, that jingle
bought you a drink." And he laughed and slapped
his knees and looked over at Buddy who held his
hands together, his two index fingers extended gently against his lips, his face still with contemplation,
and then he said, "Boy," and he put a hand on my
knee, "your legs are right there." And I began to
say something: I began to tell him that the song
was written about a true story, not about me, but
about someone else who had lost *his* legs, and about
this woman who was blind, but he shushed me
and said, "Boy," and I nodded at him, "your legs
are right there." Then he tapped my leg again and
said, "God damn," and he whooped and hollered a
little, and laughed. Then he chugged his Lone Star
and said he'd be in touch. My mom followed him
out, saying, "You sure you're not hungry, we'd love

you to stay for dinner?" But he graciously declined, climbed into his F-350 and drove away, my mom waving him down the road.

/ / /

The algebra bully walked up during passing period. The gangly guy from the bathroom was with him, and Lucy and I were leaned against our lockers. It was almost Christmas. I was wearing a sweater.

"What's a matter, kung fu?" he asked. "Ain't got a dick of your own? Gotta peep to see one?" The gangly guy laughed, but then Lucy laughed louder. A broken, crazy kind of laughter. She looked at the bully. "Whip it out," she said.

"What?" he asked.

"Whip it out," she said, and the bully stared back puzzled, and then Lucy said, "Your dick. Pull it out, and Nelson will pull his out, and we'll compare."

"What?" he said.

Lucy put her face right in his face. "I want to see your dick," she said.

The bully looked at the gangly guy, and the gangly guy shook his head. Short confused shakes.

"I'm not showing you my dick," the bully said.

"Is it little?" Lucy asked.

"Shit," said the bully and he grabbed at his cock.

"If it's not little you shouldn't be afraid to," Lucy said.

"Listen," he said. "I'm not showing you my dick in the hall."

"No one cares, if that's what you're thinking," Lucy said. "No one's gonna tell on you," then she looked up and down the hall and shouted, "Will anybody tell if this guy shows me his dick?" and someone screamed nope and everyone else was quiet. "There you go," Lucy said. "You've got nothing to worry about," then she chewed on her pinky nail, and looked casually away from him. "Unless, of course," she said, "you do."

Then the bully got all huffy, but what was he going to do? It's not like he could hit Lucy. So he just said, "Man, fuck this bitch," and then he and the gangly guy started to walk away, but of course Lucy yelled, "Not with that little dick you won't." And then the whole hallway was laughing.

/ / /

My father flung the door open and danced inside and he sort of sang, "Good news, good news, good news," on his way to the shower. I sat near the table strumming my guitar, and my mom was there listening to me, because she'd started listening to me ever since Buddy'd come by. I was working on a new song about Lucy. About the first time I'd seen her down at the bay. My mom didn't like that she had to be naked in the song, but I told her that it was true, and that true was the best thing you could be, and then Dad came into the kitchen in his towel, again swabbing an ear. "Grandma," he screamed, "Grandma!" And my grandma hollered back, "What, what?" And then I heard her walker click clacking towards us.

My father yelped back, "I want you to be in here to hear this."

It took a while for her to make her way to the kitchen. "Well," she said, a bit out of breath, her wrinkled face red from exertion. "I'm here."

Then my dad looked around at us smiling. It was quiet. "What is it?" my mom asked.

"Buddy," he said, and a grin took his face. "He says Nelson's got a chance."

And my grandmother started clapping, and my mom said, "What?" I didn't say anything. I just cradled my guitar.

"Nelson," said my father, his face aimed at my mom. "Buddy thinks he could make it," he started kind of bouncing up and down, "says he wants him to come out to the family ranch and play in person for his brother," then my mom was standing and bouncing too, and my grandmother continued clapping, and she was smiling so proud at me, "this weekend," my father said and he sprung up livelier, "wants him to meet George Straight," and he was up and down like a pogo, "do you hear that boy?" he asked me, "did you hear what I said?" up and down, "you're gonna meet George Straight," he yelped, "you're gonna play for George Straight," and then he took one great pounce and reached his hands to the sky, and when he came back down his towel slunk to the floor, and he was naked there, puny and gray, a whisper of his manhood wrinkly between his legs. He reached quick for his towel, pulled it back onto him, and then gave me a huge hug. "I'm so proud of you, son," he said, and he pulled me tight to his damp body, and I knew as my face sunk into his wet flesh. I'd never struggle the same as my dad did. I'd never have to cut meat or wash it off me. It didn't even matter whether or not I ever learned algebra.

Boy's Town #2

*No one did anything. Those ladies have diseases. We
sat drinking in the dingy room. If you were there in
the daytime you'd most likely convulse. Christ, those
are vampire conditions. Music from untuned guitars.
We drank Coronitas. Bottled seven ounce beers. We
wanted to see if we could fit an empty inside a hooker.
We had five dollars. She rolled her eyes like we'd an-
noyed her. She put a leg on the table and raised her
skirt to her belly. "What are you waiting for?" she
asked. A small crowd gathered around us. We weren't
the only ones curious. I can't explain all I witnessed.
There were sounds but no words for them. Whatever
I saw was sort of erased from my eyes. Anyhow, I'd
rather not dwell on the details. The best I can say is:
it's snug, but it goes.*

A Brief OK

White folks never dedicate their cars to loved ones. It's something I missed about back home. You'd be at a red light and look up, and the tinted window of the car in front of you would be emblazoned with a white decal showing love for the departed. *In Memory of Jesus "Chuy" Rendon,* it might say. Then under that *1978-2004.* The fanciest of the memorial stickers would be complete with little portraits, so you'd get a kind of stamp of the loved one, a sort of Andy Warhol style rendition, and those dedications always kind of gladdened my heart.

I came to McAlester to follow a boy, which is crazy because I'm not even gay. I didn't have much in the way of a life. I'd been married down on the border to a skinny little girl who smiled in reverse and was always jumping into other people's pictures. I think I got her pregnant cause a flap of grayed flesh fell into the toilet once while she peed, and we'd been drinking quite a bit the night before, and after that we couldn't even hold hands. My friend was working in the natural gas fields and he told me to hop a bus on up, and that I could stay with him anywhere and for forever, so I went Greyhound bound north through the flatness of Southern Texas—a gnarled wealth of heat and thorns—sipping whiskey in the last row of the bus with a man who spoke no English and who didn't seem to care that my Spanish was suspect, and, in a giggly haze that comes from fleeing hatred, I found my way to Oklahoma.

My friend had a little pier and beam house with a fence that was rotting, and he put me up in a back room, went off to work and dropped a barrel on his head and died. I'd only been there four days, and he'd only been there for the first two. He'd picked me up from the bus stop and we drank mightily and drove up to Robber's Cave and shot his .38 at squirrels, and we had some making up to do, because he'd dated the skinny girl before I'd married her, and our relationship had sort of tapered, and we got blind and cried and played acoustic guitar and dipped a few cans of Skoal, somehow got home and sort of laid around hungover for a day and a half before he had to go back out to the fields. He was supposed to be gone for two weeks. But he smushed his skull and stayed gone forever.

His foreman came around to tell me about it, and he had me call my friend's parents, and we cried a good deal in that awkward long-distance fashion. Great berths of static rape your ear during those kinds of conversations. If you've never talked to a mother over the phone shortly after one of their children has died, then you don't truly know how uncomfortable a silence can become. There's a death in every unspoken thought that moves through the mother's mind when they've lost their child. You can smell their defeated thoughts just burning you.

My friend's body got shipped back down to the Texas coast, and again I was on a Greyhound, this time headed south, this time sipping gin with a fat white girl in her thirties who liked cartoons, this time plagued by troubled thoughts, this time moving toward something I'd rather not face.

All my friends were at the funeral, and I did a little speech, and damned if my wife didn't jump up and hold my hand while I was speaking, and then, at the reception, while the uncles and aunts picked at flowers and the nieces and nephews skipped around uneasily, my wife reminded me that the divorce hadn't finalized, and that maybe this was a sign, but I didn't want any part of that scheme, and I was happy as hell when my friend's father called me into his office to talk with him.

This is fucked up: my friend was only twenty seven, but the bastard had a will. I didn't even have a permanent mailing address, my driver's license was suspended, and I probably needed an STD test. I sat there wanting to scratch my balls as my friend's father explained to me that I'd been left everything my friend owned. To be honest, that just made me lose all respect. The kid left me a twenty thousand dollar life insurance policy, and his house in McAlester had a year of rent pre-paid, and I could live there. I guess there wasn't a whole year left. Only eight months by now. So I sat there listening to my friend's father explain business style things with that gravelly voice the bereaved have, messing his hair, which looked washed but uncooperative, and I was like, *alright I guess I'll stay an Oklahoman a while.*

There was a lot more, but I don't remember. I ate a bunch of cookies in the kitchen with a woman who said she remembered meeting me at a party that I'm sure I didn't go to, and a cousin of mine showed up and I had him take me downtown where I rented a room on the top floor of the Omni, went down to the bars, and tried picking up strangers. I don't know, I was in the mood for something big boned. The next morning I was on another bus back to Oklahoma, this time more confused than I'd ever been on a bus, sitting completely alone drinking beer out of a thermos.

If you're like me, then you're not like most people. Especially not in Oklahoma. I spent a few months walking around drinking that 3.2 beer that doesn't get you drunk but somehow draws up a hangover, trying to meet people, but all their clothes were old fashioned and the drugs they did were derived from cold medicine, and the only books they'd ever read were in high school and had yellow pages, and the only music they heard came from the radio. If you went out dancing you'd see the strangest thing. You'd see choreography. I don't know who gets those wide bottomed girls together and teaches them about hairspray and synchronization, but there'd be forty of them wagging their fannies to the music in the exact same fashion, putting their hands on their hips and spinning in circles, their hair miraculously steady as their bodies moved in unison.

The only real friend I had was this lady I paid for hand jobs at the library. She was hideous. Her skin was near the same color as the clump of dead baby that fell from my wife's hiney, and I'm not sure how old she was, but I think she was going bald. I'd give her a twenty and she'd spank me off in the poetry section, we'd both be sitting on one of those weird canister things that you can stand on in the library to reach the top shelves, and I'd tell her about everything that was bothering me as she diddled me off—that funny flickering sound that hand jobs make. She didn't ever really talk much, and when she did it sort of sounded like she was under water or afraid that if she opened her mouth too much her bottom teeth would fall out. She was always checking out books about "horseys," and she always wanted to show me some of the pictures while she smiled. Yeah, come to think of it, she may have been a bit retarded.

I decided I needed a car, so I bought one on the cheap. I don't even know that the car had a brand. I'm serious. It might have actually been homemade by Indians who built the thing off a dare or just to show white people that such a thing could be done. I drove that rig over to Fayetteville where they have people that's been educated, and where there's a radio station at the college that plays worthwhile music, and I went to a bar that made their own beer, and it felt like a slice of something special. Northwest Arkansas smells like fresh water, and I drove over to War Eagle and jumped off a bridge, and swam around in some river, then went and had buckwheat pancakes at some kind of gristmill, pooped in an outhouse and drove on back home.

People looked at me differently when I got back to McAlester. I think they could tell that I'd been off somewhere better, and I went to a country music bar and got drunk as I could get and stumbled up to people and introduced myself, but everyone sort of rolled their eyes at me, so I started ordering shots with silly and violent names and offering them to strangers, but everyone turned me down so I had to drink them all on my own, and the whole ordeal just gnawed at me, and I decided I'd get blunt as hell. I was staring at myself in the mirror behind the bar, parts of me obscured by liquor bottles, and I was wondering what the hell was wrong with me, because the way these people were treating me you would have thought I wasn't white. After the last shot I decided fuck it—well I don't know if you decide *fuck it* but it definitely occurs to you—and I pegged the mirror with my empty shot glass, and a mob of muscly men descended upon me, and I was screaming, "Why don't you like me?" as they dragged me from the bar.

I couldn't be an Oklahoman anymore.

The guys beat me around a bit in the parking lot, but they didn't break any bones, and in the morning I went to the Pac N' Save and bought hydrogen peroxide, gauze, a poster board, a pair of scissors and nine cans of spray paint. After I soaked all my gashes in that irritable liquid that bubbles like spit just as soon as it hits blood, I started making up a stencil. I'm no artist, but I can spell fine, so I decided not to make one of those fancy Andy Warhol versions of me, and instead I just put *In Memory of Me 1979-2010*. But this operation couldn't be done completely sober, so I went to the liquor store and got a flask of vodka, pounced it with some grapefruit juice, and then I was feeling restless. I swung by the library, but my friendly lady was busy with some other guy, and I think that was nice, because I like remembering her with someone other than me—that way it can be some other monster sitting in the sound of flickering flesh with a book about horses perched on the wrong shelf nearby.

When the sun was set, I took to the streets. I don't know how many cars I got to, but I'm guessing it was hundreds of them. My stencil was nice, and after the first dozen or so cars I got good at spraying the paint so the job was completely legible. I wish I'd made another one that said something like *Fuck You McAlester*, but that's probably just anger getting in the way, because I'm proud of the job I did. When I ran out of paint I hopped in my car and headed west. Where was I going? Do I really need to tell you?

I get giddy often thinking over how that morning must have been, with all those Oklahomans coming out to their cars to see that they'd been dedicated away under the cloak of night to a person they were entirely unfamiliar with. I wonder if you went there today if you'd still see it. Surely on some of the cars. As you were paused at a red light. That mark of memoriam. And the funniest thing is: I'm still very much alive.

Corrido

The big one peeps his face out the bathroom door. He says my name. It comes out like he's under water. He waves me to him, and I go. I pause at the door. "You okay?" He shakes his head and retreats waving me in. I follow. His pants are down, and he walks wide stanced. He hands me a roll of toilet paper and bends at the waist. The fluorescents above flicker. Pale yellow light. I cough and the sound echoes off the tile. The faucet drips. Every few seconds a bead of water slurps into an open drain. The smell of shit makes thick the air. A pocket of it sits like a fist in my throat. The big one says something. A muted, impatient word. He says it again and his glasses slip from his face and strike the hard tile. He says it again, and I take a wad of paper from the roll. His heavy rump is broken with ash. It looks like flesh gone rotten after being split by a wound. He looks back at me. His cheeks jiggle, and his eyeballs strain. "Bah," he says, and his body heaves. He nods towards his ass hole. I show him the wad. "Bah," he says again, nods and then looks at his glasses that lay on the ground. The drain slurps. The wad nears him. "Bah," he says. The toilet paper brushes his skin. A sort of physical whisper. "Bah," he says again and I swallow the pockets of stench. "Bah," he says again, and the shadow of my hand flickers against his skin. "Bah," he says again as the paper skids the crack of his ass, and the drain slurps, and the flicker flickers, and I drop the paper in the toilet water, plop, and it pounces and bobs spreading out like a ghost. "Bah," he says again, and I pull a fresh wad from the roll.

/ / /

The skinny one's mother invited me to her house for dinner after she tore me a new one in front of the vice principal. This was after the first time we'd met. Every year I'm to meet with the parents to discuss student progress. This is my first year at Ronikki High. This was my first meeting with the skinny one's mother. At first she seemed nice. Shook my hand. "Name's Juanita." This was a relief. Most of the parents don't speak English. When they don't, it drags on like hot blisters, the meetings. They aim their words at interpreters, and I sit with my head in my hands. But Juanita knew English good, and she introduced herself to me and the vice principal and the Regular-Ed teacher, who sat gulping coffee, and she sat down and looked at me cold and said, "When you gonna teach my kid to spell his name?" Her kid's 21. I've known him three months.

Clearly it's my fault. She asked me a bunch of other things. "When's he gonna know math? Why come he never has homework? If he can't write his name how come he gets A's? What's he gonna do when I'm dead?" The whole time the vice cracked his knuckles, chewed his lip, and nodded, staring at me with flummoxed eyes as Juanita drilled her questions on, and the Regular-Ed teacher gulped at his coffee aloof. I had a folder with some work the boy'd done. It was mostly colorings. There were a few botched attempts at a signature, a number line that went 1,3,3,3,4,9,7, and a crude drawing of a tree with a brown leaf glued to it. "I see your concern, Juanita," I said. "I'll see what I can do," and the vice nodded. "You'd say your priority is him learning to spell his name?" I asked. I made some notes on a napkin with a marker I'd borrowed from one of the kids. "Priority," she said, and smacked the table with her palm. Then we all shook hands and left the room. Juanita chased me down afterwards and said, "Sorry I was harsh back there. Why don't you come over to my house this evening to see where Joe lives. We'll feed you. It's the least I can do to make it up, but I just always get worked up at these meetings." I scratched my beard. "I don't know," I told her. "I'm not sure what the district's policy is." A cop walked a handcuffed student down the hall beside us. The student spit on a locker. The spit ran in a streak toward the floor. "Come on," she said. "No one has to know."

/ / /

Me, "J."

Joe, "J."

Me, "O."

Joe, "J."

"No, repeat after me."

Me, "J."

Joe, "J."

Me, "O."

Joe, "J."

"No. Good try, but repeat after me."

Me, "J."

Joe, "O."

"No. I mean yes, but no."

The skinny one licked his cleft lip. He scrunched his nose and his glasses climbed his face. "I'll do it, such a good job for you," he said. "And I'm behaving so well." He rubbed his palms together.

"Yeah," I told him. "You're doing good. But say everything that I say. Exactly. Understand?"

He nodded. "Yeah. I'll do it so good for you."

"I know you will," I said. I patted his shoulder and he smiled.

Me, "J."

Joe, "J."

Me, "O."

Joe, "J."

My assistant flipped the ratchet of a pair of handcuffs he held beside him. He sat cross legged in a chair, thumping the ratchet so it coughed through the cuff. "He's never gonna learn it," he said.

"Stay positive," I told him.

He frowned and flipped the cuff again. "Delusional's more like it." He flipped the cuff again.

"Why do you have those?" I asked.

He flipped the cuff again before looking at me. "I used to be a cop," he said.

"Yeah?"

He shrugged his shoulders. He flipped the cuff again. "It's the only thing they let me keep when they fired me," he said and flipped the cuff again.

I looked back at the skinny one. "J," I said.

The skinny one dragged his tongue through his cleft. "I don't get it."

/ / /

I've been living in my sister's closet since the divorce. She rescues all manner of animals. It's why my dress shirts smell like piss. The cats have marked their territory, and they've a different opinion of the perimeter than I. To be honest I don't have a nose for it anymore. But I can see the sour in others' eyes when I stand aside them. They look back and forth as though chasing visible whispers. I know what they're thinking, "Where's it coming from?" But I like the closet enough for the time being. It's seven by seven and built of solid cedar. No hurricanes will crush me as I sleep. Plus I can talk to my sister as I lie in my sleeping bag. "How was your day?" she'll ask. "The horny one tried to stab me," I'll tell her. "Which one is that again?" she'll say, and I'll hear the springs of her mattress whine as she rolls to face the closet. "The one with the kangaroo arm," I'll tell her. "Kangaroo?" She'll laugh. "Some kind of defect. His right side's pinned back as though lifted with a string." "Like a marionette?" "No, more like a kangaroo." "But the arm still works though? I mean good enough to stab?" "No he tried to stab me with his good arm." "What did you do?" "Guys," her husband will bark, "I'm trying to sleep." He'll punch his pillow and flop in the bed. Then there will be a long silence. "I did what I was trained to do," I'll say.

/ / /

"Alright," the instructor said. "Pretend I'm visibly angry. I've got a brick in my hand and I'm pacing the floor. Pretend you've had interactions with me in the past. Pretend I'm problematic. Maybe I've self mutilated, maybe I'm known to destroy property, maybe I'm known to attack. Others. Maybe I've even attacked you. Maybe I tried to make murder upon your person. Maybe I'm the type that's in an out of institutions for damaging property, self mutilation and attacking. Maybe my attacks tend to be of the sexual nature. Maybe I'm of the disposition so as to suggest to you that I would take my rock . . ."

"I thought you had a brick?"

"So that I'd take my brick, hit you in the head with it, drag you off, and climb atop of you so as to have my way. What are you gonna do, when I approach you with my rock . . ."

"Brick."

"Brick in hand? What are you gonna do?"

"I noticed you have a brick in your hand."

"Yeah I've got a brick."

"Are you angry?"

"Yeah I'm angry."

"I can see that you're angry. What would you like to do?"

"I want to make murder with my brick."

"Oh, but that would get you in a lot of trouble. What would you like to do besides making murder?"

"I wanna run away from school."

"Oh, but we can't have you doing that. What's something you could do here at school that would make you happy?"

"I don't know. Maybe watch TV."

"Okay, we can watch TV."

"Okay."

The instructor put down his imaginary brick. "You see. Talk them down with that same method, and you will always be pleased with the results."

I raised my hand.

"Yes," the instructor said and pointed at me.

"Well I'm not sure what the big one speaks, but it's a language unreliable at best, and when the horny one gets mad he only speaks in Spanish, which I speak very little of."

"Well then," the instructor said. "Looks like you'll have to pay extra close attention in the next portion of our training procedure."

"What's the next portion cover?" I said.

"Self defense."

/ / /

The horny one stood in the door way whistling at girls. "Hello, friend," he shouted at them as they passed, his voice like helium escaping the stretched sphincter of a balloon. He waved with his kangaroo arm. His cheeks pinked. "Hi," he said, his thin voice drawing higher as he dragged the word along. He swiped his good arm at a girl with big eyes. She flinched, and his fingers just missed her shoulder.

"I noticed you standing in the door whistling at girls, when you're supposed to be at your desk, are you angry?"

"Quiet you. I stab you again." He shucked his hand at me and his head rolled as though loose.

"I can see that you're angry, what do you want to do?"

"Ah chinga tu madre, pinche mamon." He brushed beside me dragging his backpack by its handle, and it rolled haphazardly on its tiny wheels. I followed him and he looked back at me, his face shiny, his smile the color of bologna. "Ha, ha," he screamed, some forced laughter that broke apart like a burning thing. "I know what to do you." He headed for the kitchen, laughing as some enchanted puppet might, and dragging the bag that skipped behind him.

"What do you want to do?" I asked.

"Oh, shut up," he said and showed me the middle finger of his kangaroo hand.

My assistant stood aside me, he pulled his handcuffs from behind him and thumped the ratchet of the cuff, "Let me handle it, boss."

"No," I told him. "And put those things away before you get us all sued."

"Ha, ha," the horny one screamed. "I do it. I cut you head off."

"Oh, you'd get in a lot of trouble if you cut off my head," I told him.

"My mom told me I can do it whatever I want."

"Your mom didn't say you could cut people's heads off," my assistant said.

"Yes," said the horny one. He nodded his head and held his palm flat and open aside him. "I do this to my mom, the 'nother time."

"You're lying," said my assistant.

"Quiet," I told him. "Let's use the stuff from the training."

"But he's lying," said my assistant. "I saw his mom this morning and she had her head."

"I used it the glue and put it back on," the horny one said and he walked to a drawer.

"That's a lie," my assistant said. "Glue doesn't work like that."

"Quiet, you," I told my assistant.

The horny one dropped the handle of his backpack. It smacked the floor. He pulled open the drawer and his face slackened. He pulled open another drawer, and pulled a wad of hand towels from the drawer and let them drop to the ground. He pulled open another drawer and rooted his hand in it, though it was empty, "Hey," the horny one said. "Where is it the knives?"

I nodded. "I couldn't help but notice you're looking for a knife to stab me with. Are you angry?"

"I've got the 'nother thing to stab off you head with." He dug his hand in his pocket and pulled out a small pair of scissors.

"I can see that you're angry," I said. "What do you want to do?"

The horny one stepped toward us swinging the scissors as he neared.

/ / /

My assistant and I stood facing each other on a soft, vinyl mat. He reached his left arm toward me, and I grabbed his wrist with my right hand. I stepped to my left and forward, leading his left arm behind his body. I pivoted, pulling my chest to his back, keeping his left wrist clamped by my right hand. I swung my left arm around his body and caught his right wrist and pulled it toward his right hip and clamped down so his arms were slung in opposite directions across his torso, captured by a straight-jacket hold, and I dropped my left cheek between his shoulder blades and pulled my left foot back so I stood wide stanced. "Now try to pull free," the instructor said, and my assistant slung and chucked, and I was hoisted from the ground, but I stayed clamped to him, and he went back and forth, and I typewriter stepped, and we danced across the mat in oblong circles, but I kept a hold of him. "Now drop 'em," the instructor said, and I pulled my left leg farther back, then swung my shoulders to the left, and my assistant crumbled to the mat. I slung my feet behind me and spread them so we looked like this on the mat:

And the instructor said, "Now try to break free," and my assistant squirmed, slung his shoulders, flailed his feet, writhed his head, and clawed his fingers, but I just clamped, and we scooted across the mat like giant slugs. Then the instructor stood in front of us, with his legs spread wide and his arms behind his back and said, "Let me ask this. Do you feel any pain?" And my assistant shook his head no. "And let me ask this," said the instructor, "do you feel like you've got him contained?" And I nodded yes. "Try to break free again," the instructor said, and my assistant tugged at his wrists, but I kept him snug. "I can't budge," said my assistant. "Good," said the instructor. "Do you feel like you could implement these procedures if and when you have a student that becomes violent, and, in so doing, keep yourselves and your students safe?" We both nodded yes. "Good," said the instructor. "Very good."

/ / /

Left hand right wrist, the scissors, the scissors, the high bologna-stenched laughter, the scissors the scissors, arm flailing like hurricane winds, the scissors, the scissors, my assistant, "Get his arm," me, "Get his arm." Where does my cheek go, the scissors, the scissors, mouth wide open of the horny one, teeth, laughter, laughter, my assistant, "He's biting my shoulder." The scissors, the scissors. We moved through the kitchen. A chair broke. The scissors. The horny one is big and strong. "Stay on his kangaroo side," the scissors. "Ha, ha, ha, ha, ha," derangement, the scissors. Fierce red eyeballs open with veins like a cock's bulging, the scissors. Left wrist, cheek, step back. My assistant, "Other wrist, shit." The scissors. The horny one, "I do cut your heads off." The scissors. The path of our struggle:

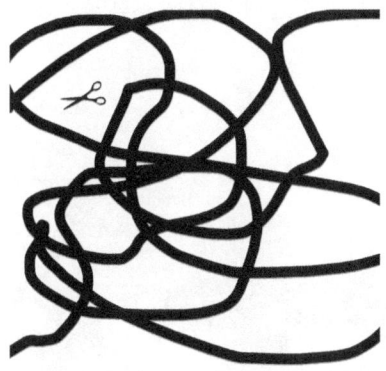

Arms, wrist, cheeks, backs, shoulders, legs, right, left, the scissors, the scissors, the broken debris from the mutilated chair, the struggle, the scissors, the laughter, the scissors. "Drop it, drop it, drop it." "My shoulder, my shoulder." "I do cut your heads off. I do cut your heads."

The horny one swung a backhanded scissor fist, and the blades of the scissors came at my face. I leaned back. I lost footing. I closed my eyes and smacked the tile. Silence. A sort of purple light. A sound like amplified feathers falling. A quick dream. Scissors dancing across a wide opened room. Their blades like legs wearing high-heeled shoes. Thirteen in total, twelve of them blue. The blue in groups of six on opposite sides a pink pair with giant red lips. The lips singing a song, the words I couldn't decipher. Then a shrill laughter and scuffing. I lifted my head. When I opened my eyes we looked like this scattered across the floor:

"You did it," I said, and my assistant smiled. The horny one shucked and kicked his good leg. My assistant clamped down. Then the horny one started crying. "Leave me alone, leave me alone." He squirmed but my assistant had him. "I'll let you go when you calm down," my assistant said. Then the big one came around the corner. His eyes widened and he clenched his fists. He screamed, "Bah!"

He stomped his feet on the floor and swung his fists through the air. He screamed, "Bah!" again, and turned his back toward us. He screamed, "Bah!" again, and then he was off and running.

/ / /

"What do you call these again?" I forked the golden brown batter.

"Sesos de cabra," said Juanita. "My mother made them," she said, and pointed at the old woman who rocked back and forth in an upholstered glider.

"Very good," I said and smiled at the old woman. She looked away from me, and ran a pinky finger through the thick mound of gray curls atop her head.

"She doesn't speak any English," Juanita said.

"Sesos de cabra," I said cutting into the fried patty, and Juanita's mother snorted.

"It's brains," the skinny one said, his mouth was full of sesos and bits of sesos fell to his plate. He swallowed thrice then ran his tongue through his lip's cleft and sucked air through his teeth. His grandmother laughed and rocked harder.

"Brains?" I said.

"Yes," said Juanita. "The brains of a goat. We raise the goats ourselves," she leaned over with one hand and raised a window. The lowing of goats floated in from the yard.

"Brains," I said. I reached for my cup and drained it.

"More tequila?" Juanita asked, and she filled my shot glass as I huffed the thick household air painted with cumin and fry grease. A kind of sweaty smell.

"I don't know that I should," I said. "I don't usually have so much."

"It's fine," said Juanita. "You're among family here."

I smiled and nipped at my Tequila. The first three shots had gone down like lava. They cooked at my insides, and I could taste the cooking in my nose. The last couple though, had been pleasant. Juanita said something to her mother in Spanish that I couldn't understand, and the skinny one clapped his hands, and I looked at him and he was smiling. Then I looked at the grandmother who was shaking her head, and Juanita kept talking, and then the skinny one was talking, and I sipped my Tequila and noticed the skinny one nodding his head, and then I nodded my head, and Juanita nodded her head, and then Juanita stood up slow, and she walked to a back room, and she talked as she moved, but I couldn't understand her, and then she rounded a corner and her Spanish was muted, and I looked at the skinny one and he said, "Guitarra," and I said, "You're funny," and then Juanita came back around the corner carrying a blonde guitar with mother-of-pearl inlays, and she dropped the guitar in her mother's lap, and the grandmother shook her head at Juanita, and Juanita smiled over at me, and she said, "My mother is going to play for you," then she said something to her mother in Spanish, and her mother whispered some words, and the skinny one said, "Um, um, um," and clapped a hand to his cleft, and then Juanita said, "Silencio," and then there was silence, and I sipped my Tequila again, and the grandmother pulled the guitar high on her lap, and wrapped her fingers around the fret board, and she flicked the strings with the nails of her free hand, and a kind of choppy waltz floated from the instrument, and the grandmother closed her eyes and sang. Her voice like a gray-feathered bird's, smooth as a memory in the center, and roughed up by tequila, and cumin, and brains at the edges. A hurt music climbed from her the way smoke flees a fire. She sang the words and Juanita translated between verses.

Ya con esta van tres veces
que se ha visto lo bonito,
la primera fue en Macalen,
en Brownsvil y en san Benito.

Juanita: With this it will be three times that re-markable things have happened. The first time was in McAllen, then in Brownsville and San Benito.

Y en la cantina de Bekar
se agarron a balazos,
por dondequiera saltaban
botellas hechas pedazos.

Juanita: They had a shoot-out at Baker's saloon. Broken bottles were popping all over the place.

Esa cantina de Bekar
al momento quedo sola,
nomas Jacinto Trevino
de carabina y pistola.

Juanita: Baker's saloon was immediately deserted. Only Jacinto Trevino remained, with his rifle and his pistol.

Entrenle, rinches cobardes,
que el pleito no es con un nino,
querian concocer su padre,
yo soy Jacinto Trevino!

Juanita: "Come on you cowardly rangers. You're not playing games with a child. You wanted to meet your father? I am Jacinto Trevino."

Entrenle, rinches cobardes,
validos de la occasion,
no van a comer pan blanco

con tajadas de jamon.

Juanita: "Come on you cowardly rangers. You always like to take the advantage. This is not like eating white bread with slices of ham."

The grandmother looked hard at me as Juanita translated. She showed her teeth before starting the next line.

Decia el Rinche Mayor,
como era un Americano,
ah, que Jacinto tan hombre,
no niega el ser mexicano!

Juanita: The chief of the rangers said, even though he was an American. "Ah, what a brave man is Jacinto. You can see he is a Mexican!"

Decia Jacinto Trevino
con su pistol en la mano,
no corran, rinches cobardes,
con un sulo mexicano.

Juanita: Then said Jacinto Trevino, with his pistol in his hand, "Don't run you cowardly rangers, from a single Mexican!"

The grandmother struck the strings firmly with her nails, and then dampened the notes with her palm. The skinny one clapped, and Juanita clapped, and I raised my glass to her and smiled. Kind of.

/ / /

The big one is fast once he gets moving. He'd hit top speed before I'd risen from the floor. I sprinted following a trail of upturned trashcans, frantic teenagers, and debris toward the cafeteria. I spotted him, his trunk-thick legs pumping beneath him, his right hand grabbing the waist band of his lowering shorts. I could hear him. "Bah! Bah! Bah!" Young girls ducked for cover, hiding their faces with their arms. I could see the policemen's eyes on him, but they stood comfortably against walls. My legs thrashed beneath me. My heart raced like a roadrunner. It was nearing noon and the halls were wound packed with students. I flittered in and out of their clusters. The big one was gaining ground. There were books and trash cans and children on the floor. I hurdled a cheerleader who sat picking up folders. "Bah! Bah! Bah!" The big one screamed, then his shorts slumped from his waist, and his ankles caught in the slumping, and he toppled, landing face down on the cafeteria floor. A crowd of students circled him. I tried my best to gain speed. I slowed when I reached the wall of backs and extended my arms like a diver, spreading the students. The big one had rolled to his bottom. His shorts remained around his ankles. Deep scrapes covered his knees in blood. I crept toward him, expecting an attack, but he saw me, and looked at his bloody knees, and looked back at me, his face jiggling near the eyes. Then he said, "Bah," and held his hands toward his knees. He barked some unrecognizable word. His lower lip slunk from his mouth. He spread out his arms. I lowered myself to him. He wrapped me up in his grip. He said the word, "Bah." I could feel his soft body rock against mine. He said the word, "Bah," and the back of my neck drew wet and hot from his tears.

/ / /

"Wake up," Juanita said.

I lifted my head from the table, smiled and picked up my shot glass. I tilted it back against my lips and a bead of tequila rolled down to my tongue.

"It's morning," Juanita said.

"Morning, morning?" I said and looked at my watch. Outside I heard a deep horn honk twice.

"Joe's getting ready for school. You should do the same."

"School," I said. I staggered to my feet and patted my pockets. My keys jangled. "Yes," I said. "I've got to go."

Juanita said, "Bye," and I waved at her and trudged toward the door.

/ / /

The vice principal and a police officer stepped through the crowd and the students fanned back. They looked down at me and I pulled back from the big one's grasp. "Everything okay here," the vice asked. I looked at the big one. "You good?" He nodded. His bottom lip still dangled flaccid from his face. "Bah," he said, and nodded. Then he showed me his bottom teeth and pointed toward his knees. "We just need some Band-Aids," I said. "He had an accident." I stood up and grabbed the big one by his hands. I leaned back and heaved him to. My back shimmied and my muscles cringed. He walloped himself to his feet, his body shirking from the thrust. We headed back the way we came. The big one put his arm around me.

/ / /

I turned the key again and the starter coughed. I turned it again, another cough. I thumped my hand to the wheel and the horn honked. My car is American made. I cursed America. I turned the key again. Another electric hacking, but no fire. No fuel? There was fuel. No fire? I stepped out of my car, slammed the door and kicked the tire. "Chief," I heard someone call. I looked over. The short bus was parked in front of the skinny one's house. Its yellow metal frame shimmied. "You need a ride?" I breathed deep the sweet stench of diesel the bus was pumping into the air. I looked at my car. I looked at my watch. I shrugged my shoulders. "As long as you don't mind," I said.

/ / /

My assistant stood behind the horny one, and the big one and I were sipping at sodas we'd bought on the way back to the room. I had an unopened soda in my free hand, and so did the big one.

"Is there something you wanted to say?" my assistant said and looked at the horny one.

The horny one shuffled his feet from side to side. "I sorry I stabbed you," he said.

"It's okay," I said. Then I handed him the soda. He smiled and rubbed his cheek against my shoulder. Then the big one handed his unopened soda to my assistant. He said, "Bah," and we all laughed. When my assistant opened his soda, fizz sprayed him in the face. Then we all laughed again.

Boy's Town #3

*That earlier bit may have been lie. Someone needed
money. We paid in part and fled. Hookers screaming
in that way only hookers can. Pockets were emptied,
but cab fare'd been squandered. We hitched a ride
with a weekend fag who spoke bad English. "Come
over to see the ladies?" we asked. "No," said the driver. "I am very, very gay." On the bridge over, putrid.
Back then you could cross in clumps. The agent eyed us.
"Bringing anything in?" he asked. I rubbed my hands.
I thought a moment. My friends all laughed when I
confessed that only a test could tell for certain.*

THE FIRST HENLEY

I know some details back and forth. The first Henley was crippled. His hands bungled by buckshot
blast. Both palms remained, but he'd lost all but
his right-index finger. It was his friend who'd done
the shooting. The first Henley was a gunman. It
was a fairly popular profession in his time. The
crippling took place up northwest in a location I'm
unfamiliar with. The main detail I know about the
crippling is this: the first Henley looked to be losing a fight. He and the man he'd dueled with had
run out of bullets, running back and forth, hiding
behind barrels I imagine, shooting at each other—
the smell of gunpowder aching the air wherever
they might have been. Each man needed the other's blood spilled. They went hand to hand once
their ammunition was gone, maybe at the center
of a dusty street, maybe in a thicket of mesquite
trees—again the specifics were never made entirely
clear to me—and they took to tussling. I don't
know if it was supposed to be all fists, or if there
existed a code in that regard, but the other man

drew a blade and mounted the first Henley. Henley was on his back with his hands to the face of the other man, and the knife came down, and Henley's best friend, a gambler named Cousins, saw that the blade would slit the first Henley's throat, and he reacted fast, firing a twelve gauge at Henley's enemy. The shot erased the enemy's face and brain, but it took most of Henley's hands in the process—I suppose scattering them as muck in many directions. After that, Henley wasn't a gunman anymore. He just wandered around with Cousins, watching his friend gamble.

Cousins owed many debts to the first Henley, and he took the well-being of his crippled friend seriously. He felt responsible for his physical state. The first Henley, from what I understand, was a lush after the injury. He'd drink often, and he wanted to die. He'd become angry with Cousins for letting him live. "Goddammit should'a let 'em cut me," he'd say. But Cousins would never deal with that question head-on. Instead he'd laugh and say, "Should'a moved your hands." This back and forth took place often between the two, and, over the years, it became a humorous exchange. Shortly after the crippling it'd be a stiff-lipped conversation they'd have—an early morning, whiskey-stained argument—but a few years later it turned into a gaffe. The first Henley might spill some coffee, the mug just fumbling from his grip. It wouldn't amount to nothing. He'd curse. "Goddammit, you should'a let 'em cut me." And Cousins' retort would come back smilingly, "Should'a moved your hands."

As far as I understand, the first Henley had achieved notoriety based on the amount of fellows he'd killed using bullets, and some of the men he'd dropped were legendary. I don't have the names. I don't think the first Henley was big enough to have comics written about him, but he was known. This resulted in two things:

First, folks were always showing up to avenge. They'd had a brother or uncle or nephew or best friend murdered by a first Henley gunshot, and they wanted him to pay for the hurt the absence brought them. In the years following the crippling, there were always people showing up and calling the first Henley out. They wanted to take him into the street and duel. This usually brought about one of two results. Some of those coming for revenge would just deflate. Can you imagine? Stoking yourself into a nervous fervor in order to revenge a loss, only to find that the fight would be grossly un-fair. The folks would just drop their heads, puzzled as the first Henley held his tattered hands toward them—a nausea from non-climax clinging their skeletons. There's something of a Stephen Crane story in that. A sort of "Bride Comes to Yellow Sky." But not all revenge seekers were well-tempered and generous. Some just saw the tattered hands as an advantage for them. Quite often they'd draw their guns, and Cousins would smoke them down. Instincts being instincts, the first Henley was alleged to wear his pistols even after the wounding. Supposedly he'd always reach for his side arms when drawn upon. His nubby hands mutely pawing the gun butts. But Cousins was a damned-good gunman in his own right, and he took care of all comers seeking to notch their guns with the first Henley's name, making bodies into masses of gore that heaped heavy on his mind. It was said that Cousins began to grow wearisome of always dueling for the first Henley's protection, that the amount of blood the first Henley brought to Cousins' hands by way of those seeking retribution was beginning to trouble his soul. It might have even been that this duty would have obliterated their friendship, but after a while word spread of the first Henley's handicap, and, eventually, the revenge seekers ceased to show their faces.

The other thing that often happened, and this endured for a spell longer than the revenge seekers—women being far less inclined to know specific details of gunfighters' lives—is that ladies would show up to proposition the first Henley. They did not show up to proposition him with sex. Well, maybe some of them showed to proposition him with sex, but more often than not what they wanted was for the first Henley to do their bidding. They had farms stolen, or husbands killed by evil men, and they had heard of the first Henley's proficiency with firearms, specifically in regards to his murdering people with them, and they sought out his services as those in need. From the way it's told, the first Henley was fairly good at recognizing these women before they'd approach him, and, always appreciating the company of women, the first Henley would try to keep his hands hid for a stretch of time, pretending to contemplate the requests of the bereft, so as to keep them alongside him as long as possible. My grandmother says she sat beside the first Henley for over an hour before she saw his missing fingers.

This was in Corpus Christi. At the time of the first Lone Star Fair. It was a failure of an event. Supposedly 20,000 circulars went out for promotion and only a few thousand people attended. There are two known highlights of the fair: it was the debut of Gail Borden, Jr.'s dried meat biscuit—a sort of precursor to his condensed milk—and the southern bad girl Sally Scull shot and killed a man in front of dozens of witnesses at the tail end of the fair—the witnesses claiming, unanimously, that the killing was done in self defense. It is most likely the notoriety of Scull's altercation that erased my grandmother's story from the greater public's memory. But she swears it's all true, and most times I believe her.

She'd come to the fair to find a gunfighter. She was naive and young, and her brother died in what she deemed an unfair fight, and she knew a handful of gunfighters' names from her brother's stories, as he was enamored with the occupation, and, until the time of his death, an amateur gunfighter himself. I imagine it was an occupation you were quick to realize either talent or failure in. She was in a saloon. A place with drinks and card playing. There, from what she understood, was where gunfighters would be. The way she tells it she had a sinking feeling before going into the saloon, because she was raised to believe that young ladies did not enter those types of establishments on principle. However, it seems to me that young ladies wouldn't travel miles and miles to obtain the services of a well known killer. I don't know all the names of all the gunfighters she knew. I have no idea who she might expect to find. I only know who she found—Murdoch Sebastian Henley.

The first Henley spotted my grandmother before she knew who he was. His name was said aloud, possibly by Cousins and possibly on command, and she came to their card table and asked if he was *the* Murdoch Sebastian Henley, which, of course, he was, and she took an empty seat beside him. The first Henley winked at the card dealer, motioned to Cousins with his head, and sat watching as Cousins was dealt another hand. "What can I do for you?" the first Henley asked my grandmother, and, because they were in company, she was forced to lean into him and speak in whispers all about her brother and what she wanted done in turn, and my grandmother says the entire time Cousins and the card dealer would snicker at each other, but that she had no idea why. She did say, however, that the first Henley just eyed her wherever. That he had no qualms with being caught staring at her womanly features, and that she'd say things such as "excuse me" and try catching his gaze with her eyes, but she sat there for quite some time, spilling her heart, begging for assistance, breathing in his ugly breath, and being looked at all over. A group of gentlemen entered as my grandmother sat at the table, and they were well-dressed and well-groomed and they had something of the dark about them, and she kept looking over at them and wondering if there wasn't a more competent gunfighter in that bunch. One that would take her money. One that would do what she needed done.

After an hour of lecherous gazing and no promises coming from the first Henley, my grand-mother decided that she was wasting her time at the card table, and she decided she'd get up and storm off. She tore into the first Henley before she left. Called him things young ladies didn't say to people—again, I imagine, on account of princi-ple—and berated him for wasting her time. Then the first Henley took his hands from beneath the table, showed my grandmother his marring, the shriveled fists flecked with scar, his one intact right index finger waving at her, and he said, "Sorry, ma'am, honest I didn't mean no harm," and he and Cousins and the card dealer truly burst into laughter then, and my grandmother was stricken a bit sick by his crippled state, and she had to lean against a barstool to steady herself and Cousins said, "Look, you've gone and made her sick," and, of course the first Henley said, "Goddammit you should'a let 'em cut me," and Cousins said, "You should'a moved your hands."

It was at this moment that one of the new dark and fancy gentlemen stepped toward the card table. "Hey," he yelled, and my grandmother, I'd imagine along with everyone else in the saloon, assumed he was about to protect her womanly honor. The first Henley even attempted to wave him off with a crippled hand and say, "We'll ease up," but the new man didn't want anything to do with the first Henley as his audience. "You Cousins?" he asked.

I can't possibly know what beef this man had with Cousins. I don't even want to assume. He hated Cousins, and he wanted him dead, and Cousins must have realized this as soon as he heard his name said, because he stood from the table and grabbed for a pistol, but he was too slow, and the new man put a bullet in his brain and heart before he'd even fully stood, and the first Henley just pawed instinctively at his own gun belt in vain as the new man walked toward him. "I know all about you too," the new man said to the first Henley, and he grabbed for Henley's right wrist, and pulled it toward him. He then took a Bowie knife from his gun belt and lopped off Henley's final finger. A swift and single slice.

This was too much for my grandmother to bear. She lost consciousness when she saw the first Henley's face clench into a shriek, and saw the gusher of blood trying to fill his fallen finger.

Later, my grandmother woke in a chair at the card table. She was sitting aside the first Henley who stared forlornly at a whiskey on the table. Cousins sat dead in the chair beyond him. The saloon was empty save the card dealer, the bartender and a few stragglers in dusty clothes.

"What time is it?" my grandmother asked. It was several hours after she'd lost consciousness. She wanted to know where everyone had gone.

I don't know who Sally Scull shot, but she shot him just moments after the first Henley lost his finger, and the entire saloon had emptied to see the aftermath—as Scull was famous, and as it was rare for a woman to shoot a man—and they had taken their numbers to another saloon, following Scull, who wasn't so much as even detained by the law, on account of her innocence being unquestionable.

The first Henley explained it to my grand-mother. His information was not firsthand. He had not moved since losing his final finger. My grandmother then realized that it was floating in the whiskey in front of him.

She felt terrible for him. He had once been fa-mous. Even she'd known his name. He was one of her brother's heroes. She remembered the boy shooting tree trunks with the first Henley's name painted on them. Not because he wanted the first Henley dead, but because he wanted to someday be his superior, because Henley was something he aspired to be. She couldn't let one of her fallen-brother's heroes stay that way. In a saloon in Cor-pus Christi watching his final finger float.

"Come with me," she told him, and, of course, she took him home, and I guess things led to things.

I don't remember much of the violent side of the first Henley. I saw him smack a wall with a nub once, but he was drunk, and there was piano music play-ing. And my father, Henley, Jr., he was a gentleman. Even the third, my older brother, he's calm as they come. So, I'll admit, sometimes my grandmother's stories about my grandfather seem false to me. They seem something made up to impress. Something she'd tell me so I didn't mind sitting beside him and letting him paw my head with his nubby hands. Something she told me so I wouldn't lose respect for him whenever I was asked to tie his shoes.

EVERYTHING WILL
FALL ITS WAY

Toby tied another string of Black Cats to the base
of the tree, his fingers working fiercely to find a
loose spot in the mound, then casually granny-
knotting the wicks together. He stepped back. His
work lay in heaps about the roots, heaved up like
dropped shoulders. There was a book of matches
in his left pocket, and he fumbled it free. He could
see the possum's eyes above, glowing yellow in the
gray light of morning. "Ugly fucker," he said and
plucked a match from the book and held it against
the striker pad.

The possum had jolted Toby earlier when he'd
arrived to open the stand—a sort of chipped up
fireworks shop at the edge of the city. Somehow the
thing crept its way in. It was rummaging a cabinet, its dirty tail dangling like a pink snake, and
that was what Toby had first seen, that reptilian
appendage flip-flopping back and forth, and at first
it didn't register, he'd even almost touched it, but
then it moved, and instead of laying his hand on
it, he banged shut the cabinet door so stiffly that

the tail came loose, fell to the floor bloody and wriggling. The possum leapt from the cabinet and out the open stand door, and Toby watched it take refuge in the tree limbs he now stood nervously beneath. He didn't want the pest there. He'd half thought about shaking the trunk until the critter fell, but he was worried it would come down upon him, so he thought maybe he could scare it down this way while standing off at a safe distance. He looked down at the piles of Black Cats. There were thousands of them.

Toby dragged the match across the rough pad and the tip caught. He leaned above the bundle of tiny explosives and dropped the flame. It sparked a wick and the bundles started crackling. He danced back grinning as the firecrackers popped and hissed, and then the pace rallied. Snap, bang, bang, like a million toy soldiers making war with tiny rifles. The smell hit Toby strong, burnt chemicals and paper, and the tree limbs began to shake, and the possum flopped from the branches, bounced in the dirt beside the exploding Black Cats, rolled up to its paws and ran awkwardly toward Toby, who shrieked, his hands flailing in front of him, yet somehow, perhaps instinctively, he reared back and sank a kick deep into the possum's face, and the thing rolled into the explosions. It tried to stagger away free but only made it a few steps before Toby, in a way fortified by the landed kick, brought another boot to the possum's side, and the animal just busted. Its charred belly blew wide open from the force—a rotten smudge of squash—and Toby looked down at the murder while the final Black Cats crackled. There was movement. Small pink and glistening things. It looked like the possum's guts were trying to crawl back up into it. Toby leaned down and sort of poked at them with his book of matches. "Sweet Jesus," he said when he realized they were babies.

/ / /

"There's not much I can think to do," the vet said to Toby who held the baby possums in a jar, their pink bodies lurched upon each other, their mouths searching for food.

"Can't fix em?" he asked, his face gray with Black Cat smoke.

"Well, see, they ain't broken," said the vet. "They just need their mother."

"I got her," Toby said, "I already showed you." Toby nudged the box again where the split mother lay in clumps of gore.

"They need their alive mother," said the vet, "and nothing's bringing that back again."

Toby turned his attention to a clock on the wall, then to a poster of a horse. "I seen a video on the computer once," said Toby, "about a cat that took care of a bird's baby," he scratched his head, "or the bird took care the cat's," he shrugged his shoulders, "think something like that might work?"

The vet looked at Toby. He looked at the jar. "I'm not sure I follow," he said.

"Like," Toby held the jar toward the vet, "you think I could get them a stand in mother?"

"Like a surrogate?"

"Sure," said Toby. "Whatever you want to call it."

The vet chewed on his top lip and rested his hands in the pockets of his white lab coat. "It's possible," he told Toby. Then he smiled, "I got some cats in the cages in the other room," he said. "We could drop one in and see how it goes." Then the vet kind of chuckled.

"I'm serious," Toby said.

"So am I," said the vet. "I just don't think you'd like the results." The vet tapped the side of the jar. "I don't think they would either." The pink things writhed.

"Hell," said Toby. "I feel awful."

"Well," the vet said. "It's a sad sort of affair." He nodded at Toby and looked at the box where the mother possum rested. "How'd you say you came to find them again?" the vet said.

"Well," said Toby and he lifted the box up to his chest and set the jar on top of it. "It's complicated." Then Toby left the vet's office.

/ / /

The large bodied car salesman kept eyeing Toby where he sat. He'd been over twice, had strolled purposefully across the storeroom and stood wide legged in front of Toby, whose head was lowered toward the jar of possums, and he'd said, "I can show you any of these cars just as good as Robby," but Toby had shaken his head, rocked a bit in the plastic chair and said, "If it's all the same I'd rather wait." The second time the salesman had looked at his watch, and looked out the plate-glass windows of the showroom storefront and said, "No telling when he'll be returning," but Toby had returned his attention to the jar and said, "There's nowhere I need to be." Then the salesman said, "What you got there? Rats?" Toby didn't look up. "Sure," he said. "Something like rats."

When Robby did return the wider salesman motioned to Toby, and Robby shook his blonde head, made his way to Toby, smiled a bright grin, and shook Toby's hand jerkily. "Well, Toby," he said. "We inking a deal today?"

Toby looked out to the lot. "There's just one more I'd like to try, if that's okay by you?"

Robby laughed. "I've never met a harder sale than you. We took out the Tacoma and there was something wrong with the suspension, next week was a Forester but you thought there were blind spots, then there was a F-150 but the interior didn't suit you. The Frontier you liked, but you didn't move on it quick enough. And the past few, hell I don't even know if you ever said what your problem was with those. You just said you needed time."

"Just want to weigh all my options."

"Yeah," said Robby. "That's exactly what you said. Weigh the options," he blinked a few times. He had the palest green eyes. They looked erased from the inside. "Well," Robby said, and he began to move toward the rack where the keys were kept, "what did you want to take out today?"

"The Land Cruiser," said Toby.

"The Land Cruiser?"

"Yes, sir."

"Is that in your price range?"

Toby nodded. "I reckon it is."

The two walked out into the lot, got to the Land Cruiser and Robby turned to Toby. "You know, most folks who come for test drives are looking to buy," he said. There was a couple looking at cars a few rows away and Robby motioned to them. "Those folks," Robby said, "they're looking for something to get their family around in. But I don't know, Toby, you've been coming here for a couple a months now, once a week or so, and I just get a different feeling off you. Some of the fellas," Robby said and motioned to the showroom where the other salesman and a mechanic stood watching from the window, "they think you might have spooky intentions."

"Spooky?" Toby said. "Spooky how?" He looked about the lot uneasily. He looked away from Robby's pale-green eyes.

"I'm not sure that I can say for certain," Robby said. "It just seems insincere you always showing up and never buying anything."

Toby nodded. "I suppose maybe," he said. "I just don't want to rush into anything. If you feel you're wasting time on me I'll understand, and if you don't want to show me this one today that's fine," Toby looked down at the sticker price. "Might be this one's out of my league anyhow," and he traded the jar of possums from his right hand to his left, and made to shake Robby's hand, but Robby looked at the jar and said, "What are those," and leaned to look, "rats?"

Toby pulled back his hand. "Something like that," he said, and he walked toward his rusted flatbed, got in and drove away.

/ / /

Thick Bob was kind of entertainment at Mc-Doogle's. He rarely had money, and the main bartender, Meredith, had a Taser Gun that she kept behind the bar for safety's sake. Once, when Thick Bob was good and loaded, he'd popped off to Meredith a time too many and Meredith took the Taser to him, thumped his fat body from the barstool in one electrifying shock. The regulars broke into unhinged laughter, because it was something Thick

Bob deserved, and Bob himself laughed as he got up from the plaid carpet uneasily. They turned this into a routine. There was a small stage in the corner, and Meredith and he would think up things that she could do to him. Once she threw a dart at him as he stood (with safety goggles on) in front of a dartboard. Once they filled his shirt and pants pockets with Black Cats that Toby provided and lit the pockets one by one. One time she sprayed him with pepper spray. Once she hit his belly with a bat. But the Taser was always the favorite, and now Toby watched from a bar stool as Thick Bob stood wincing with anticipation at the center of the stage, and Meredith held the Taser at full blast, the blue arc crackling between the electrodes, and the patrons of McDoogle's pounded their mugs in unison against their tables, egging on the endeavor, and they roared when Meredith put the shock to Thick Bob, his face seizing in pain and his fat body jiggling for two whole seconds before Meredith killed the power, and Thick Bob fell to his knees, and laughter filled the bar. Then Meredith pulled Bob to his feet, helped him over to his stool, gave him a shot of bourbon and slid Toby a Scotch and tapped on his possum jar. She frowned, "How's something so cute grow up to be so nasty?" she asked.

Toby sipped his Scotch mightily, the sip slurping aloud, as the raucous had now died down.

"Well shit," Thick Bob said, rubbing where he'd been shocked, "I seen you when you was in high school, darling, and you took a turn for the worse the same." Then Thick Bob hacked a flabby throat-ed chuckle which broke into a cough, and then he bent forward in pain.

"Fuck you," said Meredith.

Thick Bob plucked a cigar from the ash tray in front him, puffed it, and said, "Maybe when you was in high school," and broke into a painful laugh again, this time smoke aching from his gape. When his laughter faded he grumbled, "Babe, you know I'm messing."

"If you weren't I'd Tase you again," said Meredith, and she pulled a towel from the counter and began drying wet tumblers. "What you aim to do with em, Tobe?"

"Shit," said Toby, "I imagine they'll die. I took em to the vet, but he said there wasn't nothing he could do. Didn't try or nothing."

"Ever seen that video with that cat and that monkey?" said Thick Bob.

"Cat and monkey?" said Meredith.

"Yeah," said Thick Bob. "There was this cat that took care of this baby monkey," he took another drag off his cigar, "or maybe the other way around," he said. "It was the cutest thing."

"Now see," said Toby, "I mentioned something like that to the vet, but he didn't think too high on it."

"Vet?" said Thick Bob. "Doc Cooter?"

"Joey?" asked Meredith.

"Yup," said Toby. "Him."

"Well Joey Cooter don't know shit," said Meredith. "He fingered my asshole in sixth grade."

Thick Bob was wiping cigar ash off the counter in front of him, and the ashes floated down toward his lap, "Now there's a story," said Thick Bob, and he half chuckled and looked toward Meredith.

"On accident," she said. "On a dare game," she nodded. "One of those seven minutes in a closet things," she toweled a tumbler. "He was supposed to do it regular, but must've been nervous or confused."

"You wouldn't think a guy called Cooter would fuck that up," Thick Bob said.

Meredith shook her head, and smiled so her lips sunk back into her fluffy cheeks and said, "Well he did," then she took a sip from a wine glass that she had stashed behind the bar. "I think it was his first time trying."

"Well hell," said Thick Bob, "why didn't you stop him?"

Meredith sort of pursed her lips. "Don't know," she said. "Guess I was nervous too. But I tell you I never suspected that boy would be any kind of doctor."

"Ain't a good one," said Toby, "or he'd have had at least some kind of strategy."

"I got a strategy," said Thick Bob, "I'll take care of one."

"What," said Toby, "split em up?"

"It's not like they'd know," Fat Bob said. "I'll take one of em. I'll feed it something, you feed your four something else, we'll figure out what works."

Toby looked at Meredith. Meredith shrugged. Toby looked at Thick Bob. Thick Bob smiled. Then Toby tilted the jar and one of the pink possums tumbled to the bar top, its little legs limping about it, its mouth squeaking around for food.

"It's a damn precious little thing," said Meredith.

"Yup," said Toby.

"Just as precious as anything," Thick Bob said, and then he pulled his cigar from his mouth, ashed it in his tray, blew on the cherry a bit so it went red, and then he put the hot tip down on the possums head heavy, and the pink thing shrieked to a still.

"What the fuck you doing?" said Meredith, and Toby grabbed at Thick Bob's arm and flung it back and looked down at the pile of pink mottled possum, and he flicked it twice with a fingernail, but the thing didn't move. He slammed his fist twice against Thick Bob's girthy shoulder. "You killed it," he said.

Thick Bob stood from his stool. "Woo hoo," he hollered, "don't feed yours cigars," and his face went plum as he winced and hacked laughs, and he rubbed at his shoulder as he made his way out of the bar.

/ / /

Meredith sat at the edge of the bed with a paper plate on her lap, and on the plate rested the last living possum. They tried feeding them all types of food. They tried sugar-water and milk and cat food and some old bits of meat from the garbage, because possums were always getting into garbage, and they tried beer even, and coffee, and they tried little clumps of bread balled up to the size of doodle bugs, and they tried peanut butter, and chocolate, and apple juice, and saltine crackers, and the second to last one they'd given a little whiskey, and they'd tried putting them in various faux habitats, they'd set them up in the bathtub, and then they found them a cardboard box, and Toby had even let them climb around on his bare belly, but nothing they tried had worked, and one by one they were all slowing to stops, their pink little bodies just ceasing to be alive, until they got to this last one, and even it was showing signs of fading, its little shoulders less frequently heaving in breath, and its pink parts going paler, and its movements much more spare. Toby sat down next to Meredith, who had spent the night helping in every which way she was able, and who was accustomed to spending the night some, but not in this way, and the two didn't say anything until the small thing teetered out for good.

"I think that's it for him," said Meredith.

Toby tapped at the critter. "Yup," he said, "seems the life has moved on."

Meredith sort of folded the plate up over the possum carefully, stood up, and walked the paltry coffin to the kitchen where she slid the body into an empty tin of butter cookies with the others, and she put the tin of dead possums into the freezer, because trash day was near a week off, and Toby didn't want them causing a stink just rotting in the waste basket. Then Meredith walked to the bedroom door and leaned against the jamb. "I'm exhausted," she said.

Toby stared off at nothing and nodded. "I'll not be opening the stand today I don't figure," he said.

"Makes sense," said Meredith.

"I didn't mean to kill the thing's kids," said Toby.

Meredith sat on the edge of the bed with Toby and rubbed his shoulders with the open palm of her hand. They both needed to shower. Their skin and hair dingy in the sleepy morning light. "Course you didn't," she said. Her hand slowed on his back. She laughed one of those forced chuckles that seeks to be asked a question.

"What?" Toby said.

"You ever think about having kids," she asked. Toby looked at Meredith. Her face creased about the eyes, and her teeth stained by so many morn-ings spent sipping coffee. He smiled. "Got one," he said.

Meredith moved back from him. Her eyes puckering as she looked at his face. "No," she said. "Well you've never said."

"You know," said Toby. "It's one of those things," he sort of shook his head. "I wasn't even in on rais-ing him."

/ / /

Toby got his fireworks stand from an uncle who'd passed away over thirty years back. It was not an entirely lucrative little business, but Toby didn't have an expensive lifestyle. He lived in a doublewide in one of the winter-Texan communi-ties, a small mobile-home park that was near de-serted in the summer—an angry season that saw humid-highs in the low one-teens, which chased all the old timers back to Wisconsin and Mon-tana and Quebec and Manitoba. He owned the building outright, again an inheritance earned in another uncle's passing, and monthly fees at the park were only eighty dollars in the low season and one-twenty in the high, and even during bad months he'd make that in Black Cat sales alone, all the dirty-necked children of the nearby neigh-borhoods showing up in hordes on Friday after-noons with sweaty dollars they'd swap for the uncomplicated explosives, and he supplemented the income from fireworks sales by also offering a rudimentary menu of concessions (hot dogs, chips, cold cokes), food sales actually being the bulk of what he consistently brought in, and his spending was modest. He woke to generic coffee, ate mostly packaged foods, and got sloppy on well-Scotch that Meredith would pour heavy for him every night at McDoogle's Tavern. It was a Scottish pub, in theory, evidenced by the red-tartan carpet and the writing on the restroom doors—'Lads' on the men's room, 'Lasses' on the ladies—and his months and days sort of hallucinated by in modestly accented debauchery and fatigue. He was forever nursing a hangover in the heat—his tongue sticky against his teeth, and his eyelids tight to his eyes—and he was forever almost dirty, the dust from the fireworks dry on his hands and beneath his fingernails, and his clothes grayed from Black Cat paper, and a gunpowder smell that never came off. But he hadn't always been so lucky.

Years ago, back when he was young, his body still tight along the lines, and his jaw squared and trim, he'd worked alongside Thick Bob at a hotel downtown as a bellhop. At the time it was the highest-starred place to stay in town. There was a fountain in the entry that lulled sleepily and aside the fountain sat a Flamenco guitarist, perched on a wood stool, flicking strings with his fingers, and

Toby had to dress in an ivory polyester uniform highlighted by bands of turquoise, and he had to wear a pillbox hat with a gold chin strap that would chafe him, and he had to keep clean shaven, altogether well groomed, because his manager would inspect him every day, rub the prints of his fingers across Toby's face checking for stubble, and level the shoulder pads of his uniform, and pull the pillbox hat to the crown of Toby's head.

Thick Bob, who at the time was not so thick, worked as a porter. He mopped the floors and emptied the ashtrays, and he'd always come aside Toby post inspection and say, "Sure as shit glad I'm not you." Thick Bob was always around Toby and in his ear. He was lecherous toward the guests. He'd watch the women entering the hotel as he watered plants and then, when Toby would return to the entry, after having lugged the luggage away to the guest's room, he'd come to Toby and ask, "What'd ya think about that?"

"Bout what?" Toby might ask, and Thick Bob would look angrily at him.

"Don't play dumb," he'd say, "you always play dumb."

Toby would roll his eyes and look for the manager. "Don't you got something to clean?" he'd ask Thick Bob.

"Course I do," Thick Bob would say. "Go upstairs and clean that blonde woman's plate."

"That woman?" Toby'd say and Thick Bob would nod. "The one who just came in?" And Thick Bob still nodding.

"What was wrong with it?" Thick Bob would ask.

"She wasn't even pretty," Toby would say.

"That's the best part," would say Thick Bob. "You could do it all angry, and not care nothing. Fuck her in the ass and punch her in the back of the head as soon as you was done."

Toby would look at Thick Bob, repulsed by the wet in his eyes as he spoke. "Your little dick ain't fucking nothing," he'd say, and Thick Bob's face would go flat at him.

"Well," he'd say and brush a thumb across his crotch. "I might not be able to hit the bottom of the tuna can, but I can sure as shit scrape all the sides."

As far as Toby knew Thick Bob never bedded one of the hotel's guests, it seemed certain a thing that Thick Bob would have talked about if his luck brought him the opportunity. But Toby did, though just the once. It was on a Tuesday, always he remembered it was a Tuesday, because he had not been scheduled to work that evening but had been called in last minute because the other boy twisted an ankle, and he'd been drinking that afternoon, and even told this to his manager, and his manager had said, "On a Tuesday?" as if weekday drinking was an unacceptable thing, but the manager told him to come in anyhow and just not to act drunk around the guests. It was a slow evening and Toby's cap sat crooked on his head, but the manager was too flustered with filling accident reports to take notice, and he let him get away with it. A woman guest, though, she noticed. She was all alone. Toby couldn't figure why. She was older than he. Perhaps in her thirties, and she had hair so blonde it looked plastic, and it fell all about her tiny, tanned body and stayed still even when she moved, as though impossibly heavy. Her face seemed cruel. She needed help to her room. Her luggage all matched. Four bags, each smaller than the next, each red as Roman Candle fire, and Toby had flung the things uneasily where she asked him, his muscles thick in his arms like ribbons of mucus, and she had looked him over when he'd completed the task. Studied his arms, his shoulders, his face. She had even straightened his cap for him. And the whole thing just happened organic. Their faces collided, and then a tussling ensued. A split-second and violent sex emerged. She'd been wearing a dress, something with sequins, thin straps at the shoulders, and Toby had pulled those from her, and lifted her skirt to her waist, and she shimmied quick from her panties, and he chucked his uniform shirt, and let his ivory pants fall to his ankles, and then she drove him into a chair and climbed upon, grinded her body down against his, again and again, Toby's pillbox hat rattling on his head, and it only took a few dozen thrusts, he balled his fists as he came in her, and she moaned a withered gasp that somehow matched the yellow light of the room. She shrank off him, and their breaths slowed, and it was awkward. She went to the restroom and closed the door without saying a word. He got up, pulled his clothes together and scrammed.

Toby didn't see her again that evening, and the next night he took a different guest's luggage to that room—now a guilty haunted space to him—and he never told anyone about it until that morning when he told Meredith.

/ / /

As Toby slept, the truest dream. He came face to face with the sixth grade Doc Cooter, his finger buried in Meredith's asshole up to the final knuckle, the three of them in a closet that smelled of stale clothes, and Cooter looked Toby blank in the eyes and said, "Possums play dead," and then all that faded, and Toby was back in the trailer, the light some hideous hue, seated on his bed, and who should wander in, but the busted mother possum on all fours, that long snout bathed in light unnatural, and blessed with ability to speak, she said simply, "How could you?" and then all about her ambled the babies, and Toby sprang from his bed and out the trailer door, but everywhere he went the image trailed him, became the corners of his imagination, and his dream mind sent him on a search for the box that he had stashed, the one that the dead mother rested in, the one he'd placed in a dumpster behind McDoogle's Tavern, and lifting it from the blue metal box, and flipping the lid, found it to be empty, and then the Possum tapped his shoulder, "Looking for me?" it asked, now larger than it had been, the size of a man, twirling its bloodied tale nonchalantly, and Toby touched his hand to the busted belly, his fingers stained red by the wound, and then he took to running again, sprinting in fact, but every step was plagued by memory, every dim spot in the landscape inhabited by the dead beast, and he couldn't shake it, couldn't go fast enough, and moved so much he couldn't breathe, fighting for breath, haunted by possum, and quickly all things snapped from him, and he was upright awake in his bedroom and gasping for breath.

"You okay?" Meredith asked.

Toby looked around. Clearly fazed. He looked at the clock by his bed, leapt to his feet and said, "I gotta go open the stand."

/ / /

Toby remembered very well the first time Robby came to his fireworks stand. He came in a pack of other children, of which he was clearly the leader, and they bought bottle rockets for the purpose of "shooting cross the canal." Those words stayed with him. That first meeting was not when Toby suspected the boy of being his. It took years before he'd made that connection. It wasn't that Toby and the boy looked the same, it was that Toby just felt it. Robby came every Friday for most likely four or five years, and while it was clear to Toby that Robby didn't recognize him when he'd go to his used car lot, Toby couldn't mistake him for anything. Those were the palest green eyes he'd ever seen, a truly different color than Toby's, but the same color eyes he'd stared into in his mother, the woman at the hotel, who'd thrown him against a chair and had her way with him. Toby didn't go directly to the stand after waking from the bad dream. He'd gone to Robby's car lot, had stared into those pale-green eyes and promised he wanted to buy a car, and then, while they were driving, Toby behind the wheel and Robby in the passenger seat rattling off logistics of the vehicle while drumming his fingertips on the dash, Toby had said, "Mind if we make a quick stop," and Robby said, "No problem with me," and Toby pulled the Land Cruiser up to his fireworks stand, and Robby said, "Hell I've been here," and a gladness took Toby's heart. "Is that so?" Toby said. Then Robby looked at Toby, his eyes clearly studying him, "Shit," he said and pointed at Toby, "You're the fireworks man." And Toby just nodded and said, "I'm gonna buy this car."

/ / /

A few days later, there was a scare. Thick Bob had taken a bit longer to come off the carpet. He'd stayed there dazed, his body writhing a bit even after the shock ceased. The drunks at the bar even kind of gasped. It was one of those movie-set silences. All things seemed constricted. As though the whole world was choked. But it was only a momentary silencing of him. He had fallen to his back, frozen, but he shot up with a gasp, a wide-opened look on his face, and then most everyone at McDoogle's cheered him. Meredith aided him to a bar stool and took the batteries out of the Taser. "I think we'll be through with that for a while," she said.

Thick Bob stayed silent. He rubbed his head vacantly, then looked at one of the drunks who sat a table away. The man was not a regular, and he wore a terrible shock. "Hey," Thick Bob said to him.

"Me?" said the stranger.

"Yuh huh," said Thick Bob. "You know," he continued, "you need to be careful around here."

"Careful?" said the stranger.

"Yup," said Thick Bob, "cause there's a faggot in this bar."

"A faggot?" said the stranger, and he sort of looked around.

"It's true," Thick Bob said. "But," he continued, taking a bourbon from the bar and sipping daintily at it, then staring at the new man, looking him up and down, "if you give me a kiss, I'll tell you who it is."

The stranger laughed uneasily, then sipped at his beer. Thick Bob winked at him and turned back to the bar. He again rubbed his head. "There was something," he said, his face going vacant. Then he looked at Toby, "I brought you something," he said.

"Brought me something?" said Toby.

"Yup," said Thick Bob, and he reached beneath his bar stool and thumped a hefty book to the bar.

"A book?" said Toby.

"It's a ledger," answered Thick Bob. "Meredith told me about your ordeal."

Thick Bob had stayed on at the Rivera Hotel even after Toby'd gone away. He was still employed there, though he'd never graduated from porter, or perhaps he'd elected to keep the position, as it grew increasingly easier for him as the hotel lost distinction, and as he was somehow predisposed toward occupations that called for skimp responsibilities. The story struck Thick Bob curiously, the details redelivered to him with great specificity, and after Meredith told him he let himself into the Rivera Hotel office, found the log book for the first year he'd been employed there, the only year Toby had worked alongside him, cross referenced an accident log where he found a report for a twisted ankle filed the same year, and found the exact Tuesday evening when the lady guest had checked in. The one Toby had slept with. Hillary Olsteen. Room 183. Which Toby could not remember the room number of specifically, but once Thick Bob explained the exact location of the room, sort of mapped it out on a bar napkin with a felt pen, Toby agreed it had to be the same, and that this must have been the woman. But hearing the name did not leave him feeling secure.

"What good is it knowing that?" he asked Thick Bob.

"Well," said Thick Bob. "Just figured you'd want to be sure. You think you got her packed with seed. Seems to me if I had that suspicion I'd want to look into it all, just to be certain."

Toby did not like the name in mind. He looked at Meredith. She glanced at him and then away. Then Toby stood and left.

/ / /

It took a few days for all the financial matters to be organized, and Robby had the Land Cruiser cleaned up to near mint before Toby came in to finalize the purchase. He watched Robby hover above several forms, a pen in hand, a tightness to his posture. He was speaking. An almost foreign language. Financial jargon and mechanical issues, dull and hollow words that rolled lifelessly through Toby's brain. He'd other things on mind. How could he pose the question? It all felt ignorant to him now.

He held in his right hand a Styrofoam cup of black and acrid coffee which he'd nearly polished off, and now he swirled the final swallow at the bottom, so it seemed a critter chasing itself. "Toby," said Robby, and Toby looked up from his cup. There was a question about adding a warrantee, and Toby declined, as it cost a couple thousand dollars, then he said, "How's your mother doing?" And Robby looked slightly puzzled and said, "My mother?" Then Toby told a lie. He said he remembered her bringing him by the stand some and Robby said she might have done, and he tried to redirect the conversation back to the matter of the Land Cruiser, but Toby wouldn't let it. He said the name. "Hillary." But a silence followed. Robby eyed him. "Hillary?"

"Your mother," said Toby.

"Stacy," said Robby. He reached into the top left drawer of his desk and pulled out a portrait in a black plastic frame. It was of Robby some several years prior standing in front of some woman strange to Toby's eyes, and aside a man that looked near identical to Robby, though some many years his senior. Toby took the portrait from Robby and puzzled over it.

"Not the woman you were thinking," said Robby and smiled. "Now we're all about done," he said, "just a few final signatures."

"I don't suppose," Toby said. "That you were adopted."

Robby laughed a sort of forced and crinkled laughter. He worked side to side in his seat, then took the photo back from Toby. "Not at all," he said.

Toby looked off at a nothing. He felt soft. Made a fool. Something hideous swallowed him empty. Robby made to hand him a pen. Held it in his polished-fine hand. Smiled the cleanest smile beneath his ornamental eyes. Toby looked at the pen. He looked at Robby. "I'm having," Toby said, "second thoughts."

Toby couldn't quite remember all that happened after that. His exit was blurry to him. But he could recall, as he walked away, that Robby yelled at him to never return.

/ / /

That night Toby's sleep was demonized by troubled dreaming. He could not place the nature of the terror, but there was an ever present panic that forced him scrambling in mad directions through his unconsciousness. Some dreams are like that. They are terrible for no given reason. He rose clammy from his slumber, feverishly looking for the cause of his haunt, as though somehow it had woken with him. It was early in the morning. Hours before the sun would rise. Toby got dressed and went out to the garbage, which he had dragged down to the curb just before going to sleep. He lifted the lid from the can and pulled out the butter-cookie tin. He pried open the container. The four possums were still partly frozen, their carcasses made gooey from the thaw. It was not the right way to leave them. Toby placed the lid back on the tin and he climbed into his flatbed. He drove slowly down dark deserted streets, the hum of streetlight muddled in the humid early hours. He drove straight to the fireworks stand. He somehow knew he should. And, once there, he knew to go inside, to take four rockets from the back cabinet and place them near the spot he stomped the mother. Toby had chicken wire in the stand. He'd give bits of it to children, actually teaching the technique he now used to bind the possums to the rockets. The four little beasts, partially frozen and bound, like miniature crucified things, the rockets made taped to sticks that Toby pierced in the dirt. Moonlight made them glisten as though toys. Toby struck a match. He was able to get all four wicks with one go. Each wick hissed as it caught. And then, when they ignited, the rockets spit skyward with a scream, a plume of white smoke coughing them away from the earth, and they sailed up that way, climbing away from where Toby stood, and the rockets, one by one, bursted into fits of color, oranges, greens and blues, embers falling so gently, explosions that marked the spots where the possums would have made their way back down to the ground, and wherever they landed is where they stayed.

Slug Trail #2

Some things removed will follow you back in glisten-
ing trails you can trace toward the ghoulish deeds left
done. You can step into the same river twice. Larger
still, that river can step inside you. Swimming to your
center. A current unforgiving. As if to say, "You might
leave me, but I'll barely ever leave you."

Brian Allen Carr lives and writes in Texas. His fiction has appeared in *Annalemma, Boulevard, Fiction International, Hobart, Texas Review* and other publications. He is the winner of the inaugural Texas Observer Story Prize, as judged by Larry McMurtry, and his first collection, *Short Bus,* was a Steven Turner Award Finalist.

www.ingramcontent.com/pod-product-compliance
Lightning Source LLC
Chambersburg PA
CBHW030637130626
46552CB00002B/896